The Little Buddhist Monk
&
The Proof

The Little Buddhist Monk

&

The Proof

•

CÉSAR AIRA

Translated by Nick Caistor

A NEW DIRECTIONS PAPERBOOK ORIGINAL

Copyright © 1998, 2006 by César Aira
Translation copyright © 2017 by Nick Caistor

Originally published by Grupo Editor Latinoamericano, Argentina, as *La prueba* in 1992
and by Mansalva, Argentina, as *El pequeño monje budista* in 2005; published in conjunction
with the Literary Agency Michael Gaeb/Berlin

Manufactured in the United States of America
First published as a New Directions Paperbook (NDP1378) in 2017
New Directions books are published on acid-free paper
Design by Erik Rieselbach

Library of Congress Cataloging-in-Publication Data
Names: Aira, César, 1949– author. | Caistor, Nick, translator. |
Aira, César, 1949– Pequeño monje budista. English. | Aira, César, 1949– Prueba. English.
Title: The little Buddhist monk & The proof / César Aira ; translated by Nick Caistor.
Description: New York : New Directions, 2017.
Identifiers: LCCN 2017000429 | ISBN 9780811221122 (acid-free paper)
Classification: LCC PQ7798.1.I7 A2 2017 | DDC 863/.64—dc23
LC record available at https://lccn.loc.gov/2017000429

10 9 8 7 6 5 4 3 2 1

New Directions Books are published for James Laughlin
by New Directions Publishing Corporation
80 Eighth Avenue, New York 10011

Contents

THE LITTLE BUDDHIST MONK

I

A LITTLE BUDDHIST MONK WAS ANXIOUS TO EMIGRATE from his native land, which was none other than Korea. He wanted to go to Europe or America. The project had been incubating in his brain from his youth, almost since infancy, and had colored his entire life. At the age when other children were exploring the world around them, he was discovering a longing for distant worlds, and what he saw around him seemed like the misleading image of a reality that awaited him on the other side of the planet. He couldn't really remember, but he could have sworn that even before he knew of Europe or America, he already wanted to go, as if he had been programmed within to receive the calls of faraway places. At any rate, his ignorance, if that is what it was, did not last long, because his earliest reading was geographical, and later on, studying the cultures of the countries he dreamed of took up more of his time than his religious training, which in the order he belonged to was extremely demanding. Intelligent and obstinate despite his diminutive size, he enjoyed a distinguished career as a monk while at night he studied languages, history, philosophy, politics and psychoanalysis, in addition to reading Shakespeare, Balzac, Kafka and anything else worthwhile. Our little Buddhist monk was living proof of the saying: "Knowledge takes up no space."

Of course, this intellectual preparation only solved half the problem, and the second half at that; the first part, that of practicalities, remained unresolved. To start with, he had no real possibility of saving the money he needed for the airfare. And over there, in the dreamt-of First World, he didn't know anyone who could find him a job to support himself. More seriously still, he had no idea what kind of work this might be. He was not equipped for any kind of profession, at least not the conventional ones. He was not unaware that every so often Buddhism became fashionable in one or another of the western countries, or in all of them at once; and he knew that the people in those countries most likely to follow these fashions were members of the well-heeled classes. They would pay handsomely for a genuine article like the little Buddhist monk. In fact, he knew of quite a few compatriots who had successfully exploited that seam. But they had done so as part of institutions that organized the journey, accompanied them, installed them and lent them legitimacy. Unfortunately, the order he belonged to was extremely local; it did nothing to promote itself, was against teaching outside the group, and detested all institutional organizations. So much so that it was a misuse of language to say that he "belonged" to the order, since once they had completed their studies, its members were left to their own devices, without teachers, monasteries or rules. They were wandering mendicant monks or, if they so wished, they were sedentary, public preachers of independent means; in short, they could be whatever they wished without anyone holding them to account. They had no way of recognizing one another. It was possible that they were all equally determined to emigrate but didn't know it, and each believed he was the only one. It was possible they were all of equally reduced physical dimensions as the little Buddhist monk, but didn't know that either.

To have a project can help make life liveable, and it doesn't matter how unattainable it might be; quite the opposite in fact, because if that is the case, its influence will be all the more absorbing and prolonged. Practical people say that dreams serve no purpose; but they can't deny that at least they allow one to dream. The dream of a journey had endowed the little Buddhist's life with meaning. Without it, his existence would have been lost in the capricious inconsequentiality of contemporary Korean history and, tiny as he was, his efforts would have been wasted. Thanks to the project, all his studies and readings complemented one another; none was wasted. Someone might ask: what do studying Hegel, reading Truman Capote, poring over the plans of the châteaux of the Loire, and delving into the struggles for power between Guelphs and Ghibellines, Tories and Whigs, Republican and Democrats have in common? These might seem to be fragments of disparate areas of knowledge, and in anybody else they would indeed have simply fed a pointless curiosity. In him, they were all directed toward a common goal. Practically no leap of his agile mind, whatever discipline he applied it to, failed to contribute to his ultimate goal. In a word, the project had given his life direction, and if it seems unnecessary for someone in the Far East to find a direction, just imagine that if the East exists, it is because on the other side there is the West, and it was precisely this that caused the little Buddhist monk so many sleepless nights.

But one day his dream would come true, he thought, as he raised his eyes to the sky in which he glimpsed the distant reflection of the skies awaiting him. "It costs nothing to dream," he told himself. And if reality was defined by its identification with itself, he glimpsed in that inverted overlap of antipodean skies the triumphant congruence of dreams and life.

II

THE ESCAPE ROUTE PRESENTED ITSELF UNEXPECTEDLY one day in the shape of a French photographer who was visiting Korea. As well as being unexpected, it was extraordinarily casual, as the vagaries of fate tend to be. Lost in his daydreams outside a luxury hotel, the little Buddhist monk was almost knocked over by a couple who were suddenly spat out by the revolving door. With a rapid maneuver—a leap to one side and two or three hasty steps—he managed to avoid being trampled on. He was accustomed to this kind of dodge: a sixth sense warned him of the danger, while his strolls through the busiest parts of the city produced such a plethora of incidents of this kind that they became a constant weaving from one side to another. His tiny stature meant that not everyone saw him, but even if they did, it wasn't easy for them to calculate the consequences of their respective movements, since one step for a pedestrian of normal size was equivalent to five for the little Buddhist monk.

The man and woman who emerged from the hotel were extra large. He was fat and as tall as a basketball player. He was weighed down by a capacious backpack, climber's boots, trousers patched with a multitude of stuffed pockets, and a jacket that gave away his profession. She was scarcely less big, with ash-blonde hair, horsey features, red hands and thin lips that failed completely to conceal the braces on her protruding teeth. She was wearing an elegant man's suit. From the summit of their corpulence they did not even spot the presence of the little being they had been on the point of crushing, and they would have left him behind in a second if they hadn't altered course and headed for the curb. From their gestures it was plain they wished to hail a taxi. Had it not been for this change of direction, which obliged the little Buddhist monk to take evasive action a second time, he would have returned at once to his daydreams and continued on his way, repeating his zigzag progress further through the crowds. And he would have done so anyway, if at that very moment one of the couple had not uttered part of a sentence in a language he knew. The words were, I quote, "*quelqu'un qui parle français,*" which doubtless referred to their debate about which taxi to take. They must have wanted (how naïve!) to be driven by someone who spoke their language.

Then, before the story could resume its fluid course of events, there was one final moment when chance had to choose between what did happen and what might have happened. If the little Buddhist monk had thought about it for an instant, if his mind had even fleetingly taken into account his timidity, his insignificance, or the general pointlessness of everything, he would not have opened his mouth. But as this was not the case, he pronounced the words that complemented what he had heard: "*Moi, je parle français.*" He failed to realize that what he had heard might only be part of the proposition. "Someone who speaks French," could be the conclusion of a phrase along the lines of "Let's hope we don't have the misfortune to bump into someone who speaks French." Which only goes to prove that sometimes it's better not to think.

When the French couple heard this unexpected but fitting reply, they were taken aback. They must have thought for a moment that they were faced with a supernatural phenomenon, which they could have put down to the immanent magic of Korea. It is only natural that tourists, especially when they travel really far, lose all sense of proportion in their expectations, or are content to set out with a delicious, tantalizing vagueness, as if to allow for the possibility that the strangest things could happen. And to a European, the furthest East is naturally a world of enchantment. This moment lasted rather longer than it should have, because when they peered around, they could not see a soul. Had the voice come from somewhere inside themselves, from the mystery of their marriage? The lack of an accent added to their doubts. When they finally spotted the little Buddhist monk they smiled and greeted him, still rather shocked.

This tiny incident was the beginning of a mutually beneficial relationship. The little Buddhist monk immediately sensed that his opportunity had arrived. But the opportunity for what? In a flash, as if he were about to be hit by a train, he saw it all. A rich French traveler (it was a luxury hotel), for whom he could act as a guide, show him his worth, become his irreplaceable assistant, and by means of subtle diplomacy, win the favor of being taken with him ... Beyond that, which was no more than a spark of his imagination, was the life he would lead in Paris, the fire this spark would ignite. He was astonished. It was as though it was only at this moment that the project to emigrate was born, and it exploded with such force that it gave a retrospective glow to all his previous life, endowing it with a meaning that until now it had lacked.

III

THE FIRST AND MOST IMPORTANT CONSEQUENCE OF this chance conversation by the sidewalk's edge was that the French couple gave up on their idea of taking a taxi. Because they had to admit they didn't have any precise destination, or rather they did have one but did not know where to find it (this obscure point was soon cleared up). The apparition of this "providential man" as they called him, even though they recognized that the phrase sounded strange when applied to someone so tiny, spared them this unnecessary wandering.

They discovered that they had lots to say to each other, far too much to remain standing there buffeted by the flood of people crowding the street at that time of day. After some hesitation, they invited him to a café: on the one hand they were uncertain whether as a monk he was allowed to enter this kind of establishment, and on the other they did not know whether in Korea there were cafés where people could sit and chat (they had only just arrived). On a more subliminal level, their doubts also sprang from a fear of offending him, since as a result of the difference in their height, when they spoke to him standing up they had to lean forward, and it might seem very impolite to invite him to sit down simply to be level with him and avoid a backache. By then, after the initial exchange of pleasantries, they considered him too valuable to offend in any way. They had only just met him, and were already afraid of losing him.

The little Buddhist monk swept aside these fears at a stroke when he said that of the many cafés they could choose from in the neighborhood, he recommended one that was just around the corner. They went straight there. It really was very close. As they entered, the French couple admired the decor; they thought it was very like *Les Deux Magots*. The same dark wood paneling, the old leather chairs, the partitions with beveled glass, the shiny brass. At that time of morning there were few customers. They ordered coffee, and began to talk.

The Frenchman was called Napoleon Chirac. He was a freelance photographer: he didn't work for any agency, and did not accept commissions. He regarded himself more as an artist than a conventional photographer. His camera had taken him around the world, from Australia to Canada, according to his whims or his inspiration. While he didn't avoid the exotic, it was not the focus of his searches; on the contrary, he explored the exotic in order to reveal its ordinariness.

An image hunter? asked the little Buddhist monk.

Not exactly. However odd it might seem, images were not his objective, or were only a by-product. His work was with spaces.

Spaces? What did he mean? And how could one speak of

spaces in the plural, when space itself was one, a single, continuous and all-embracing whole?

He was referring to human spaces, or rather the way that different cultures compartmentalized space. For example, the alleys of New York, the museums in the Old World, football stadiums . . .

The list could have been endless. The little Buddhist monk gave in to the temptation to demonstrate his wit, despite knowing full well that wit always runs the risk of being excessive or inappropriate. But this time he hit the spot:

Dollhouses?

Napoleon smiled and looked at his wife. No, he had not tried with dollhouses. It hadn't occurred to him, perhaps because it would be difficult with his method of working. "Difficult" but not "impossible." He would have to use a special lens. It might be worth the effort.

This observation led to a momentary change of topic. The little Buddhist monk had proved so intelligent that the two foreigners' attention turned to him. And since they found it impossible to ask why he was so intelligent, they questioned him about something as close as possible to that: how had he come to speak such perfect French? Had he lived in France?

This was a good opportunity for him to express his desire to emigrate, and yet he preferred to leave that for another occasion; he was certain there would be one. For the moment, the little Buddhist monk responded with a white lie: he said he had taken conversation classes at the Alliance Française. Then he cleverly redirected the conversation back to its previous course, taking up again a point that had been mentioned but not elaborated on: what was the Frenchman's "method of working"?

It consisted in photographing a "space" from its center, covering the whole perimeter in a series of linked images. Then he made a digital "join" which produced one single landscape-format photograph.

The little Buddhist monk nodded. He understood. It was ingenious, although it might not be all that original; he thought he had seen something similar, if not the same, in an art magazine. But he didn't say this. Napoleon Chirac was opening the backpack he had placed on the bench beside him. He took out an oblong box about twenty-four by eight inches and began to lay the photos in it on the table.

He explained that this was his latest project: dance halls in Havana. Recalling his earlier explanation, it was not hard to interpret them, but even so they had a strangeness about them that made them interesting. The montage of the different images was perfect. What they showed were empty rooms, some of them with tables and chairs, a piano, or a platform or stage, a bar, doors, windows. At first glance the image looked like a single photograph taken with a wide-angle lens, but closer observation revealed distortions in the perspective and besides, it became obvious that the shot was too wide. The left- and right-hand edges coincided at exactly the same point; if either picture had been even a few inches longer, there would have been a repetition, and although this would have made reading the image easier, it would also have revealed the trick.

Napoleon showed him a dozen or more of these images. They were in color, and printed on very glossy paper; the dance halls, some of them bigger than others (although it was hard to tell) were sordid and sad, contrasting sharply with the strange air of luxury lent by the mechanism of straightening out the circular shape. None had any people in them. The little Buddhist monk asked if this was always a deliberate choice.

Which indeed it was, in all the series. Only when there was no piece of furniture to suggest the human scale did he introduce an isolated figure to suggest the dimensions ... At this point there was a short silence, one of those polite pauses the French couple would have to get used to with an interlocutor of the unusual size that they had stumbled across.

Well then: after the Havana dance halls, he had wondered: now what? And decided ...

One moment. Forgive the interruption, but how did he choose the themes? Because after all, there were "spaces" everywhere. Without needing to quote Pascal and the "miseries of mankind" that came from "the inability to sit alone in a quiet room," it had to be recognized that the house one lives in is also a "space."

Yes, that was true, but the idea was to explore culturally charged spaces. And the photographer's vocation had always been that of a traveler. How did he choose his subjects? As he had already said, whim and chance were part of it. He found his subjects through reading, films, TV documentaries. Sometimes he just set off on an impulse, or went in search of one thing and discovered something different.

What about now? Why Korea?

His current project involved Korea's Buddhist temples.

On hearing this, the little Buddhist monk raised his eyebrows. He thought for a while, glanced at the long photographs spread over the table, thought about it again, and nodded. Napoleon Chirac smiled, relieved and content. With good reason: it was important to him to get the approval of an intelligent local who after only the briefest explanation had understood what he was trying to do.

I have to warn you, said the little Buddhist monk, that the temples you're going to find here are not enclosed spaces.

The Frenchman already knew this. On this occasion it was not a random voyage, although every trip has something unexpected about it that made it worthwhile. He had done his research, and this openness of Korean Buddhism to nature was the challenge that had led to his choice.

Did he have a particular temple or temples in mind?

He took a tourist map of the country out of his backpack and unfolded it. He showed him photographs of the temples of Bulguksa, Sinheungsa and others.

What do you think of them?

There are other less touristy ones. If you will allow me, I could guide you.

This was what the French couple had been hoping for, and they leaped at the offer:

Seriously? Would you be so kind? It would be such an invaluable help to us. Would you have the time to spare? Aren't we interfering with your duties?

I have absolutely nothing to do. And even if I did, I could think of no better use of my time than to serve an eminent artist and to enjoy the company of an educated, delightful foreign couple with whom I can practice my poor French.

Many thanks. How kind. We ought to agree on an adequate financial compensation ...

Not at all! he interrupted the Frenchman. I'll do it for the pleasure and honor of doing so. This is where sacred duties of hospitality and the most elementary patriotism coincide. Besides, the order I belong to forbids me to receive any monetary reward. I don't know if you noticed, but my apparel doesn't have any pockets.

The French couple were delighted. They couldn't believe their luck. The little fellow was giant-sized.

IV

TO CELEBRATE THEY ORDERED A BOTTLE OF CHAMpagne. No one could deny it was worth it, because they really did have something to celebrate. Even so they hesitated for a few moments, because they were aware that to drink champagne in the morning was a bold statement. When asked, the little Buddhist monk declared that he had no objection to alcoholic beverages. And among these, rather than a cheap sherry or a run-of-the-mill whisky, Napoleon Chirac, who was making the choice, was inclined toward what was after all most logical. Champagne had the exact symbolic resonance that the moment called for, and was appropriate above and beyond the symbolic, since it was a good aperitif; and besides, it was no longer that early in the day.

But when they raised their glasses in a toast, the French couple froze in surprise. The "clink" of the glass captured a snapshot of their astonishment. The only thing moving were the tiny bubbles inside the glasses, and it was precisely these bubbles that were the object of the foreigners' rapt attention: instead of rising, they descended, going from the surface of the liquid to the bottom, where they fizzed about in crazy swirls.

By now entirely assuming his role as a national guide, the little Buddhist monk dismissed the supposed miracle with a laugh. Instead he gave a perfectly rational explanation: they should not forget that they were on the far side of the world, and the magnetic poles were reversed.

In addition, he went on, as they sipped their drinks, in general Korea had something of the "world upside down" about it. Not so much in its practical, visible aspects as in certain mental structures. In fact, the country's modernization that followed from contact with western travelers and traders in the sixteenth century had been the by-product of a religious polemic that had its roots in a strange inversion.

The French couple drank in his words. His French was so perfect and elegant it sounded prerecorded. Encouraged by their close attention, he explained:

The conflict had arisen between two branches of Buddhism who were arguing about the way to tell jokes. One of them, innovatory thanks to western influence (and which ultimately was triumphant) proposed telling them with the punch line at the end. The other school resisted any change, and defended the traditional Korean way of telling them, in which the punch line or climax should come at the beginning, not the end.

An example? Of course. The innovators proposed:

I have no legs. I'm a snake.

Whereas the traditionalists argued in favor of the ancient way, one that had made so many generations laugh:

I'm a snake. I have no legs.

The little Buddhist monk readily admitted that this example might not help clarify things much. It was not for nothing that one of the two schools of thought had won out, and for centuries had shaped the mental categories that were part and parcel of the perception of the joke. From the vantage point of the present it was hard to understand the virulence of the passions aroused by this debate. One had to take into account the force of habit, and the ancestral creation of expectations. That was what it was about: the role of people's expectations. What also needed to be taken into account was that the controversy took place in a religious context, so that jokes were not jokes in the modern sense, but parables with a spiritual significance.

However, the undisputed, complete triumph of the modernizing school, which gave Korea its place in the modern world, had not led to the disappearance or forgetting of the ancient way. On the contrary, its persistence as a mental substratum was what made jokes funny.

How strange all this is, said Napoleon Chirac. It gives one such a strong impression of having left the normal world behind and of being on the far side of the looking glass.

The little Buddhist monk responded to this with a conciliatory smile: it wasn't that big a deal. Globalization, so reviled by nationalists of every stripe, had led to greater communication, which meant that previously unnoticed inversions were lent greater contrast and meaning.

Korea, he said, had not only taken but given. A great exporter of products with high added value and cutting-edge technology, it had become respected throughout the world as the supplier of the most demanding consumer goods. And it has also exported a valuable human resource, in the substantial emigration of a disciplined, hardworking labor force, enterprising traders, small business owners (and big ones) who have established their picturesque Korean neighborhoods in every city around the world.

And, turning to a specific point that might interest them, Korea also exported art. From the most serious kind, the art of museums, of which one eminent example was Nam June Paik, whose work they surely knew—they agreed—to the most popular forms of entertainment such as the amusing cartoon about SpongeBob SquarePants.

Was SpongeBob SquarePants Korean? They thought it was American.

It was true that now it was promoted by a North American company, but it was created in Korea, and was in fact a typical Korean creation. It still bore traces of that even after the distortions it had suffered at the hands of western cartoonists.

Moreover, he went on, in the genesis of SpongeBob SquarePants there was an echo of the old controversy about jokes. Did they know what the cartoon was about? It showed the adventures of a boy sponge and his friends, the starfish, the squid, the crab who owns a fast food restaurant, the little diver squirrel ... Well, the original idea was to have this character live either on the bottom of the sea, which is the natural habitat for sponges, or in a bathroom, in the little porcelain niche above the tub where human beings interact with sponges. In the latter case, it would have been an example of the traditional kind of joke from Korean folklore, with the resolution coming before the development. However, due to pressure from the North American TV channels, the other format was adopted, with the result that the climax of the joke would have to come at the end (the logical end) of a vast poetic saga that was both almost infinite and also very convenient from the commercial point of view.

The French couple were fascinated by this torrent of information, of which their tiny friend seemed to be an inexhaustible source. Since by now they had emptied the bottle, they ordered another one, and took advantage of the pause to change subjects. Napoleon Chirac picked up the tourist guide that had been left on the table and opened it in the middle once more, at the pages devoted to the famous temple at Bulguksa, a standout tourist attraction with three stars.

So you are of the opinion, he said, that it's not worth a visit to Bulguksa? Won't the series be incomplete without it?

Of course you must go there! exclaimed the little Buddhist monk. Of course the series would not be complete without the supreme diadem of the treasures of our Korean temples! What I said was that there are others which are more interesting because they are less well-known or celebrated. But Bulguksa is a must, it's unavoidable, like the Eiffel Tower or Times Square.

And in fact, he went on, Bulguksa had successfully withstood tourist vulgarization. It could make a good subject for his photography, especially sectors such as the platform of the main shrine in the complex, Daeungjeon, where the two famous pagodas were placed.

The shrine was built in the second half of the eighth century by a prime minister, Kim Daeseoing, who was a follower of Buddhism. He had the two temples built in memory of his parents, and this could explain the differences between them if it was true, as tradition had it, that one was dedicated to the father, and the other to the mother. They are placed symmetrically on both sides of the square, though all the charm comes from their lack of symmetry, because they are very different from each other. The "motherly" or "feminine" pagoda, called Seokgatap, is the lower of the two (twenty-seven feet) and the simpler. It has three levels, and is elegant and austere. The name Seokgatap means "the pagoda of Sakyamuni," the historical founder of Buddhism. Its construction represents the spiritual ascension following the rules imposed by the Buddha Sakyamuni. The symbolic idea is that this ascension is relatively easy if one adheres to the dogma. And perhaps it also means that this is the path recommended for women, who should not concern themselves with any great intellectual complexities but pursue the established rules obediently.

The other pagoda is called Dagotap, which means the "Pagoda of a thousand treasures." It is taller (thirty-four feet), more solid, and much more elaborate, with eaves, cornices, balustrades, doors and windows. Its baroque style symbolizes the complexity of the world, whose "thousand treasures" are mankind's ambition.

There exists a legend about these two pagodas that might interest you, said the little Buddhist monk.

Of course it would. The more he spoke, the more interested they became. This was both automatic and inevitable: had this not been the case, if their interests had already existed separately from each other and had to collide, it could never have happened. It would be like the Buddhist tale of the turtle that sleeps on the sea floor and swims up only once every hundred years. It can appear anywhere on the immense surface of the oceans, while also somewhere in that vastness floats a ring that is four inches in diameter. How probable is it that, as it pops up, the turtle's head will pass through that ring? How long will one have to wait before that coincidence occurs? It is just as unlikely that what someone says should coincide with the interest of the person they are talking to. (The modern version of this turtle is SpongeBob SquarePants.)

The legend says that one morning a dead horse appeared in the square of Daeungjeon. It was flattened against the floor tiles, its spine crushed, skull smashed and brains spattered all around. It had obviously fallen from a great height, which explained the noise heard shortly before dawn by the monks now gathered crestfallen around the carcass. In their semiconscious state they had thought that part of the temple had collapsed, but the Buddha sent them so many dreams at that time of morning that they had preferred to stay in bed.

The monks knew the dead animal. It was an imported Chinese pony that was tired of life and wanted to commit suicide. Its lack of knowledge of Korean botany meant it could not find the toxic herbs that could have brought its existence to a discreet end, and so instead it decided to throw itself into the void from the highest point it could climb to. In the region, there was nothing higher than the two pagodas at Daeungjeon. But how could it reach the top? It's not easy for anyone, still less a horse, to climb the outside of a steep building, to practice architectural rock climbing. One has to realize the importance in Buddhism of the number of legs each living being has: an importance even greater in this case. With two legs (man, partridges) the climb would not have presented any great problem; with many (a centipede) even less; with four, it was mission impossible! Despite this, the horse's determination to end it all was so great that it set off on the climb. It chose the Seokgatap, which although it was slightly lower seemed to present fewer obstacles. It was an infinitely demanding task. Clinging desperately to the cornices, its hooves slipping everywhere, its round belly dangling to one side and its haunches to the other, in a clumsy imitation of Spiderman, climbing one inch and sliding back three, head down, curling up into a ball, folding and unfolding like an electrician's stepladder, the horse sweated and panted upward for hour after hour. The monks recalled having heard during the night an irregular series of scraping sounds, thuds and snorting; they had attributed this to a flock of storks mating in the temple roofs.

Finally the desperate pony reached the top of the pagoda, and without giving it a second thought launched itself into the air. As it fell, at that supreme moment when everything was already decided, it saw it had made a mistake, and that rather than scaling the Seokgatap it had climbed the Dagotap. Instead of making things easy for itself, it had made them difficult. And during the instant of the fall it had time to reproach itself for this lack of attention, and to think that perhaps it was this failing that had led it to despair of life.

What a beautiful, sad story, the French couple commented, and what a rich message it must surely contain for anyone who can correctly interpret it.

V

THEY HAD BEEN TALKING SO MUCH THAT THE MORN-
ing sped by and, whether it was because they wanted an excuse
to continue their conversation sitting down without having to
start work, or because the champagne really had worked as an
aperitif and had opened their appetite, the French couple suggested they have lunch together. They did so tentatively, admit-
ting they did not know at what time Koreans ate, or more im-
portantly, what plan of action the little man might have devised,
since they had tacitly left it up to him.

Amply justifying their decision, the little Buddhist monk
took charge. Yes, it made sense to go and eat, and to have a
good lunch so that they could devote the whole afternoon to
photography. He had already decided on the temple where the
distinguished visitor could make his first foray: one that was in
the vicinity of the city, easily accessible by train, not often visited but very characteristic.

They at once paid and left. The little Buddhist monk hur-
ried along in front of them, saying he knew a nice place nearby
where the food was good and there was no problem getting

a table. He set off through pedestrianized alleyways, and the French couple followed without losing sight of him, admiring the ease with which he slipped through the crowd of people who could not even see him. Although they paid close attention, they were always on the point of losing him, because he was rushing along so quickly at ground level, and so many people kept getting in their way. This pursuit gave them little time to see where they were going, but that was not important anyway, as they would never have been able to get their bearings: the narrow alleys became a real labyrinth. They turned to the right, then to the left, then right again, while at the same time the streets also turned right and left; they crossed roofed-in sections, one of which housed a bookshop, turned left and right again, and there they were. A set of very worn marble stairs led to a creaking glass door through which they entered before they could even glance at the front of the building or the signs outside, which they could not have read anyway.

It turned out to be a Greek restaurant, not a Korean one. The owner greeted them effusively and led them to a table. Only when they were finally seated did they get the chance to look around. They found themselves in a squarish room that was higher than it was wide, with about twenty tables covered in white paper cloths, heavy china plates, tin utensils and chunky glasses. Dark wooden beams stretched across the ceiling, and hanging from them, defiantly incoherent, were a great many crystal chandeliers. None of them was lit; what little light there was came in through the front window from the narrow street outside. The walls were lime-washed blue, with several small, garish oil paintings hanging from them.

Curious as all this was, it was nothing compared to the owner. He was a hyperactive, loud, middle-aged Greek with a very dark complexion, intensely black curly hair, thick eyebrows, sideburns and mustache, and a checked shirt with the buttonholes bulging across his paunch. Even though there were two waiters, he busied himself at every table, shouted out all the orders, and when there weren't any, sang snatches of Italian opera in a deep voice that made the air quiver.

He took their orders, which they had deciphered as best they could from a menu written in three languages: Korean, Greek and Italian. They asked for a mix of baklava, goat stew (highly recommended) and bean soup, with a bottle of the house red. The food was good and the atmosphere, once they became accustomed to it, was welcoming. They soon fell into conversation again.

The little Buddhist monk, who for his own ulterior motives knew how important wives were, turned his attention to Napoleon Chirac's partner, who until then had remained discreetly in the background. Her name was Jacqueline Bloodymary; she appeared to be about the same age as her husband or slightly older, did not dye her hair or wear makeup, and was very French.

Turning toward her with a friendly gesture that signified both "at last we're going to talk about something interesting," and "I didn't ask before simply because I was unable to, because your husband took center stage," he inquired what she did for a living. The pleasant smile she responded with showed she had understood the intention of his gesture. Her satisfaction came not only from the pleasure of having understood this gesture, the intellectual contact that was the basis for civilized interaction, but also from her realization that there was room (and more) in a person of such reduced dimensions for gestures with such a variety of meanings.

What did she do? was his question. Did she merely collaborate in her husband's work and accompany him on his travels, or did she have her own interests?

Her reply came as a great surprise to him, a rare occurrence as Buddhism usually shielded one against shocks of any kind.

I am a ... cartoonist.

A cartoonist? She had smiled as she said this, and hesitated a little, as if the word might have more than one meaning. The mysteries of language.

But she had not meant to create an enigma or have him guess what she meant. She explained at once, accentuating her smile—that is, making it look serious.

She drew "cartoons" for tapestries.

The little Buddhist monk mentally flipped through the folders in his memory archive, and came up as intelligently as ever with:

"Aubusson?"

No, not quite. It was a dream of hers to work one day for the famous tapestry makers, but at the moment she did so for more modest manufacturers, family firms or old village workshops that needed to update their designs. She was aiming for Aubusson, but had no wish to rush her apprenticeship, like a writer who learns to write a novel by writing short stories.

But that must be poetic work, even if it were considered as a stepping stone toward a more artistic endeavor. Especially since she could never tell what the final outcome would be.

He was right: it was like writing film scripts. What counted was the idea; that was what she was paid for, and she felt like an inventor. In her case, it was a visual idea.

Where did she get her ideas?

Where did she not get them from! At one time she had let her pencil roam over the paper for entire afternoons (endless notebooks) and then chose from this ocean of doodles some short black lines where something new, suggestive or mysterious had been registered.

The little Buddhist monk, raising eyebrows that were themselves short black lines in a suggestive and mysterious drawing, expressed his admiration at the procedure because it appeared so simple.

Really simple! Whoever said work should be hard? It was enough to choose one's work well and then choose the easiest way to do it.

Over time though, she had given up this "automatic writing," although not entirely: she had moved on to another kind of automatism, that of chance encounters between shapes in the real world, and their faithful reproduction in drawings. Of course, this did not mean she had renounced abstraction, because when these drawings were cut up, inverted, or superimposed on one another, they went back to their state as signs suggesting ideas.

After that came a third stage, then a fourth, and a fifth. There were always new ones. The main aim of this change of method was to learn and gradually acquire the capacity to draw the idea directly without any intermediary.

The tapestry weavers repeated this "idea" endlessly. In fact, for them a single idea could suffice for a lifetime.

Jacqueline had taken a pencil from her bag and had been illustrating her words on the white paper that served as a tablecloth. Joining up all the little doodles with a few skillful strokes, she produced two lines that looked fractal and represented the opposing outlines of the two pagodas, as she had imagined them from the description the little Buddhist monk had given. The space between the two pagodas, ingeniously illustrated, formed the shape of a falling horse.

VI

BY THE TIME THEY LEFT THE RESTAURANT IT WAS MID-afternoon. The little Buddhist monk suggested they go straight to the temple on the outskirts of the city, the one he had suggested would be ideal for them to start their work. Unless they had to return to their hotel first to pick something up … No, said Napoleon Chirac, he had all his gear in his backpack, he never left without it. But he was worried about the time. Wouldn't it soon be nightfall? He had to remind the little Buddhist monk that his method of working was extremely time-consuming as it was the painstaking representation in space of the time it took to complete a 360-degree turn.

The little Buddhist monk dismissed these fears with a decisive wave. He said the Frenchman could never before have found it so easy to perform this turn and capture the suspension of time from the inside. Besides, far from being a waste of time, their little trip was perfect, since anyway they had to wait for the light, the famous Korean light, to become less harsh: by the time they got to the temple it would have reached exactly the right point of velvety density, and from then on would only gain in depth, reaching the summit of the photographic ideal.

He sounded overoptimistic, but said all this with such con-
viction that it made the French couple want to go and see. And
since this was why they had come, and as they had nothing else
to do, they followed him.

They set off back along the narrow alleyways, hurrying after
the little figure who glided along at ground level. Slightly uneasy, they wondered who exactly they were following. If they
had to explain, what would they say? That they had run into
the smallest man in the world? Or would they need to say "the
smallest Buddhist monk in the world"? It would be unfair to
reduce him to his physical dimensions, because they had been
able to appreciate his intellectual and human capabilities, and
something like a friendship had grown up between them. They
understood him perfectly, and yet in some (indefinable) way
his size still gave rise to doubt: who exactly did they understand
so well? How? Following him along these narrow streets, which
were a chaotic mixture of East and West, was like following the
genie of tourism; an impression only strengthened by the fact
that nobody but them seemed to see him.

When they reached the station, which really was very close,
they could transfer their attention away from their guide and
take a look around. There were so many people heading in so
many directions that the little Buddhist monk slowed down,
turned toward them, and suggested that they stick close to each
other to avoid getting lost. Was it the rush hour? Here, all hours
are rush hours.

The station was an amalgam of ancient and modern. This is
true everywhere, but here it was even more striking because the

modern was ultramodern, with cutting-edge railway technology stuck like a collage on to the ancient. And the ancient was itself very old indeed, dating from the first days of train travel, a time when such modes of transport were ultramodern, too modern to replace the horse.

They found the ticket office. Napoleon Chirac went up to the window; behind a thick pane of glass, an impassive Korean man spoke to him in Korean through a microphone. His discreet lip movements did not coincide with the sounds emerging from the speaker. The Frenchman realized that not only did he not understand him, but that he didn't know what to say to him either, as he had no idea where they were going. From down below came the helpful voice of the little Buddhist monk telling him the name of the station that was their destination. He made him repeat it, because he found the devilish pronunciation of oriental names hard to follow. As he had to look down to perform this short dialogue, the ticket clerk, who could not see below the customer's chest, probably thought he was either consulting the ground itself, or a little dog. Eventually he was able to say the name of the station and held up three fingers to show that he wanted three tickets. At the same time as the clerk said something incomprehensible, the little voice down below shouted: "No, two! Only two!" A moment of confusion followed, since the Frenchman was obliged to carry on two dialogues at once, so that while he persisted with the incomprehensible station name (varying his pronunciation slightly) and still held up his three fingers, he also said to the figure below him: "Why two? Aren't you coming with us?"

This worried him, as it meant a change of plan. And as more unintelligible words poured from the speaker, the voice below explained that Buddhist monks traveled for free on the Korean railways. So Napoleon began to signal with two fingers, bending the third back into the palm of his hand.

Once the problem had been resolved, they went past a huge number of platforms, from which trains were constantly departing. Some were bullet trains, made of pink metal and aerodynamic in shape; others were old and dilapidated, pulled by steam locomotives. Theirs was somewhere in between, the carriage walls made of wooden trellis work. But their carriage was quite ordinary, without compartments, and with seats covered in turquoise-colored plastic.

On board the train, the crush of the platforms was transformed into impeccable order. All the seats were occupied by men in dark suits with briefcases, or women in ironed, brightly colored dresses, office workers returning home as smartly dressed as if they were just starting their day.

There was a whistle, and the train pulled out. If the French couple had been hoping to get a panoramic view of the city, they were disappointed, because no sooner had they left the platform than the train entered a long, dark tunnel.

Is this an underground train? they asked, when they saw that the tunnel showed no sign of coming to an end.

The little Buddhist monk replied that they were only crossing the Rocky Wall that separated the upper neighborhoods of the city from the lower ones.

They closed their eyes, bored at seeing nothing but darkness, and drowsy from their meal and the range of emotions and impressions with which the first half of the day had bombarded them.

When they opened their eyes again, they saw they were speeding through chasms, over bridges suspended between vertiginous heights or steep mountainsides, or ledges at dizzying angles. As far as the eye could see—and it could see very far—all of this was part of a vast mountain range dotted with forests, lakes, sunken valleys and tall peaks. In the incessant hairpin bends made by the tracks, they alternately saw the locomotive puffing up an incline, or the guard's van sliding down a descent; on one side a peak rising into the clouds; on the other the tops of centuries-old pines covering a distant valley floor. They became slightly alarmed: weren't they traveling too far? They had understood that the temple they were heading for was on the outskirts of the city ...

The little Buddhist monk reassured them: not only were they still in the city, but they were not far from the center. What they could see was a park, a nature preserve.

A park? But it's immense!

He said it wasn't that huge. It appeared more extensive than it was, due to the high mountains and the vertical perspectives.

It was volcanic terrain, which in the remote past had undergone violent folds and transformations.

Civilization had tamed it, turning it into Sunday afternoon walks in the fresh air, secluded nooks for lovers, and backyards for childish antics. A proof of its moderate size was the fact that mothers sent their children to play there in the time between their coming home from school and their evening meal. When they wanted them to come in, all they had to do was lean out of a window and give a shout. As they gazed out at the vast landscape stretching to the horizon, the French couple could scarcely believe it. They asked what the place was called.

The Mountain Park ... of Korea, replied the little Buddhist monk, with a slight hesitation that he immediately concealed by pointing out some of the park's attractions: the highest and lowest peaks, the darkest forest, the lightest, the valley of clouds, the deepest lake ...

Why is there nobody in it?

It must be because of the time of day.

It's a privilege for all these people, said Napoleon Chirac, to come home from work in the evening and to be able to enjoy these majestic surroundings. The soul rejoices at the sight of all this grandeur.

He was about to add something more when an incident distracted him. A gentleman, a typical Korean bureaucrat who was seated slightly in front of them on the far side of the aisle, suddenly stood up and pulled the white cord that ran beneath the luggage rack. The train braked at once, with a loud screeching sound. The door between their carriage and the one in front opened and the guard came in at a run. He started arguing with the man who had pulled the cord to stop the train. The French couple looked to the little Buddhist monk for an explanation, or at least a translation. Instead of complying, he merely pointed at the carriage window opposite them. Outside, a station platform had appeared. This seemed to them to explain the incident: the passenger must have wanted to get off there, and when he saw that the train was not slowing down, he had pulled the emergency cord.

But why then was the guard still trying to convince the passenger with words and gestures that he should not get off the train? In any event, he was unsuccessful: the bureaucrat had clutched his briefcase firmly and was striding toward the door, deaf to the other man's exhortations. When they looked out of the window again, the foreigners thought they noticed something strange about the station; not only was it deserted, but it looked too simple, like a makeshift stage set; it even seemed to them translucent. The train pulled out of the station, and they saw that the passenger had indeed disembarked, and was walking along the platform.

The little Buddhist monk gave an irritated sigh. His reaction was enough to dissuade them from asking any further questions.

However, soon afterward the same thing happened again. This time it was an elderly lady dressed in a parrot-green tailored suit who stopped the train by pulling the cord. The guard appeared once more, there was the same argument, with the same result. Since this time the station had appeared on their side, they got a better view of it, and were convinced it was not real. It must be some kind of hologram. They commented to each other that the projector might be on the carriage roof ...

The little Buddhist monk interrupted them with another sigh, this time a weary one. It wasn't a projection, or at least not of the kind they were imagining. There was nothing for it but to reveal something he would have preferred to pass over in silence so that they wouldn't think ill of his country; but anyway, it was quite harmless, almost ridiculous. The deception had begun when he told them the name of the park. In full this was: The Mountains of the Witches of Korea. The fact was that, according to popular tradition, this area was inhabited by witches. Of course, nobody had ever seen any, apart from the inevitable few madmen and visionaries, and the witches' questionable existence was only revealed in the effects they produced. These were as gratuitous as they were unpredictable, although over time they had become almost routine. The witches were pranksters; the recurring trick they seemed to love was to take over the mind of a passenger on the train that crossed their domain and induce them, in a hypnotic state, to stop the convoy and get off at some point or other along the route, a point at which there momentarily appeared the semblance of a station that was their illusory "destination." After the victim alighted, the station disappeared within a matter of seconds, and so did the hypnotic state, leaving the poor passenger with no other recourse than to walk the rest of the way.

The "prank" was repeated in exactly the same way on each train. It didn't amuse anyone, except for the "witches," who apparently never grew tired of it. There were many complaints to the Western Railway, and there had even been lawsuits. The guards had received orders to do everything they could to convince the hypnotized passengers not to get off, apart from using force; and although they never succeeded, they always followed the regulations.

The French couple asked the little Buddhist monk what the rational explanation was for this phenomenon. He shrugged his shoulders. Suggestion, superstition, the "real dreams" of a nation that lived in dreams, who could say? It might also be some kind of metaphor employed by a population alienated by modern life, by their routine jobs and lengthy working days, to express the boredom of their journeys back home, or their dependence on the cruel chance that ruled the functioning of public transport and city life in general.

This left the French couple pensive. The train continued to climb and descend mountains. In the white and golden distances the world became mist and the mist became world. The blue peaks rose like the boundless borders of a concave landscape.

VII

A RED ARCH FRAMED THE ENTRANCE TO THE SHRINE. Once they passed beneath it, they had to follow a winding path which rose and fell, and was lined with trees and flowering shrubs. Sometimes the vegetation appeared wild and untouched; at others it seemed cultivated by keen gardeners. From the high ground they could spot the roofs of the shrine up ahead. To either side, beyond groves of trees and hedges, they could see meadows, lakes, stands of bamboo, and ancient lonely trees that stood like giants on the lookout, as well as an old wall that also rose and fell almost parallel with the path, but now to the left, and now to the right. In the silence, the birdsong was loud and clear, with such a variety of different calls it was as if the birds had gathered from all latitudes and continents for an international competition.

Their guide had been telling the truth when he said they would not be bothered by tourists, because there were no visitors to be seen. Here and there solitary monks strolled along or stood stock still to contemplate a flower or empty space. They neither greeted nor looked at them, but something about their self-absorption led Napoleon Chirac to think he and his camera might not be welcome. Would the temples even be open to the public?

Wouldn't they need special authorization to photograph them? He reproached himself for not having asked before. They had touched on so many things in their conversation, and yet this fundamental point had escaped him. Striding along the path in front of them, the little Buddhist monk seemed certain of a good reception, but maybe he took it for granted without having checked. After all, he was a monk, and so it was logical that he should have free access to all the temples he took it into his head to visit. But perhaps he had never been to one accompanied by foreigners.

Well, there was no point creating so many problems for oneself. If they didn't allow him to work, he had not missed much. He could regard it as an agreeable walk that had taught them a lesson. But they would have lost a day. Without being able to explain how it had happened, Napoleon's thoughts had taken a pessimistic turn. The atmosphere of the place continued to suggest that things wouldn't be so easy.

He glanced out of the corner of his eye at Jacqueline. She was walking with obvious delight as she admired the vegetation, breathing in its perfumes, and doubtless making mental notes for her cartoons. He tried to copy her carefree attitude and enjoy the moment. It couldn't be that difficult; all he had to do was recover the optimistic mood he had been in for most of the day.

However, in order to recover it, didn't he first need to work out what had prompted it? The key obviously lay in their providential encounter with the little Buddhist monk the moment they'd stepped outside their hotel to breathe the Korean air. Providential in the extreme: bumping into a native who spoke French, knew everything, someone they got along with and who had offered to be their guide. All the problems of a journey to distant lands had been resolved at a stroke. Wasn't there something magical about it?

My word, but there was! So why not continue to trust in that magic? It was very easy to do, because it had not been exhausted by their initial encounter. Napoleon realized there was an extra element that made everything even more special and was still having its effect: the physical size of the little Buddhist monk. Something as trivial as an excess in dimensions—in this case, a negative excess—was enough to suggest that he was supernaturally effective.

No sooner had Napoleon formulated this reassuring line of reasoning than he saw something that plunged him back into confusion. A monk appeared some way off at a bend in the path. He was absorbed in the contemplation of a spiderweb. And the fact was that this monk was astonishingly little. The Frenchman's dismay was immediate. If there were other monks this small, the magic of "his" was lessened. He looked from one to the other. Even if the distance prevented him from properly estimating his size, the newcomer must have been about half as tall as an average man. Of course, this still left him considerably taller than the little Buddhist monk. At the risk of stumbling on the uneven ground, he continued to stare, and it seemed that this monk was even a little bit bigger than he had first calculated. A rapid glance at their guide reassured him completely: "theirs" was definitely smaller. He must have been confused by the identical nature of the terms he was using, because this temple resident was also a "little Buddhist monk": nobody could deny that he really was small. In addition to being a relative term, "small" was a very broad term, very "big" in its own way. And if there was still any doubt as to how correct his estimation was due to the distance, it was a doubt in their monk's favor, because distance makes things smaller.

The tranquillity that this reasoning, which passed through his French mind as rapidly as a bolt of lightning, suddenly came to naught. This was because no sooner had the first monk disappeared from his range of vision than another one appeared, equally immobile and concentrating on some thought or other: and he was much smaller than the previous one. Napoleon roughly calculated that he must be half the size, although he did not want to exaggerate: this one was further away from the path and was standing in a hollow, or perhaps on a hillock; it was hard to calculate. Whatever the case, he was strikingly tiny. Was Napoleon to conclude that in Korea the vocation of Buddhist monks was reserved for people of reduced size? If that were so, the sense of enchantment produced upon them by the little Buddhist monk was simply due to their ignorance as foreigners; they would have to rethink the way they had adopted him as a magical spirit or talisman. While considering this, Napoleon looked ahead once more and had the pleasant surprise of confirming that "his" little Buddhist monk was still smaller, like one of those legendary champions whom the new generations of competitors try to surpass but cannot. He screwed up his eyes (but there was no point concentrating hard on this isolated figure, because that only made him seem larger), then quickly turned his head to superimpose his outline on that of the other monk. But that one had disappeared behind a hedge, or perhaps the path had turned a corner.

At that very moment, to complete his mental confusion, he spotted a third little monk also standing lost in meditation (apparently they had nothing better to do), also tiny. Except that he was much smaller; Napoleon thought he was about half as tall as the second one, and the first one now seemed to him enormous. In his bewildered state, he was unable to decide whether this monk was much further off than the previous ones, or much closer. He tried to get a good view of him before looking away, because he suspected that he was going to disappear as soon as he had taken a few more steps, hidden behind a shrub or some such. He did not take long observing him, because he needed to keep an eye on the little Buddhist monk, who was striding ahead of them. He was relieved to see yet again that he was smaller still, incomparably smaller. But if new monks from the temple kept appearing who were smaller each time, wouldn't one eventually beat him?

The Frenchman tried to get this stupid game out of his head. He had no idea why he had started it in the first place.

What did he care if there were bigger or smaller monks? But it wasn't so simple. Once he had embarked on this speculation, it wasn't easy to return to the starting point and not set off. It might be easier to take the speculation to the opposite extreme, and get out of it that way. He made one last effort in this direction: maybe the monks he had seen were one and the same, seen from varying angles and distances: given the winding nature of the path, this was not such a farfetched idea. If this were so, it would explain his sensation that, however small they were, they would never be as small as their little Buddhist monk: the reduction in size due to distance is never that deceptive, thanks to the automatic corrections the brain carries out.

Another explanation could be that they were not real monks at all, but statues, like the cement gnomes that people put in their gardens, statues of the temple's ancestral *bodhisattvas* whose different sizes represented their level of importance or illumination. And of course, these two explanations were not mutually exclusive.

Napoleon Chirac recognized that it was childish of him to cling to the belief that his little Buddhist monk was the smallest Buddhist monk in the world, and yet in every artist there is a remnant of childhood not assimilated into the adult personality, like a sea horse in a human-shaped tank, or like a talisman that allowed him to enter all the temples and take all the photographs he wished.

VIII

HIS WORK SOON FREED HIM OF THESE STERILE FANTA-
sies. Despite the particular direction that he had followed
within his profession as a photographer, which had more to do
with phantoms than realities, the process was a more concrete
manipulation of reality. And because he was still uncertain how
much time he would have, in spite of the little Buddhist monk's
assurances, he set to work with a certain urgency. What a contradiction: he was abandoning a desperate attempt to prove to
himself that he had come across someone who could manipulate dimensions as if by magic, only to almost instantaneously
reject the assurances about enchanted, suspended time that
this same being had made. But this wasn't really a contradiction, or it should be said that realism was a contradiction in itself. The flowers from a lemon tree are not lemony, and yet its
leaves are! The less realist a work of art, the more the artist has
been obliged to get his hands dirty in the mud of reality.

No one prevented Napoleon Chirac from placing his tripod
wherever he wanted, nor the camera on the tripod, or the photoelectric lighting cells all around him. The kind of photography

he believed in made it necessary for him to decide first and fore-most where the central point was. But before he could do that, he had to work out what circumference most interested him. He let himself be guided by intuition, refined by his practice, and rectified by his taste. He had discovered that in nature there was no such thing as a circumference. It was the occasion that created them.

In general he chose a point off-center, so that the circle would open out. The center of the temple looked a bit like one of those raised open bandstands common in European parks. It was made of wood painted dark red, with a very low roof and half-surrounded by a balcony supported on slender columns. On one side was the shine, which was dark apart from a bronze Buddha gleaming at the far end. On the other, a dwarf stone pagoda that did not obstruct the view of the park. And in the background (but it would also be in the photograph) stood the monks' tumbledown dwelling.

Paper decorations hung from all sides of the circular roof. There were more in the entrance to the shrine and inside it, as well as little paper lanterns in the nearby trees. The impres-sion was of an untidy, gaudy children's birthday party. The pop music blaring out of loudspeakers everywhere only added to the sensation.

Is this a day of celebration? he asked the little Buddhist monk.

No, it wasn't. But as is well-known, for Buddhism "every day is Christmas."

The paper decorations and the lanterns were of bright,

lively colors, mostly red, although the rest of the spectrum was also well represented. Some of them were spherical, and these most resembled the balloons of children's parties; others were shaped like pagodas, flowers, or Chinese letters. Most of them though were round or long concertina shapes, clustered together in different-sized bunches; these were what set the overall tone of the decor. They were swaying gently in the breeze, and all looked brand-new. Could the monks have so little to do that they spent all their time making them and putting up new ones every day?

The photographer was bewildered. He was unsure whether he had won the lottery or was wasting his time. The old wood from which everything was built and the views in the background of nature both wild and cultivated could not have provided a more striking contrast to this lamentable party atmosphere. But that was what made it exotic.

At least he could not complain about the light, which seemed to him perfect. He looked at the small tablet on which he received the data from the cells he had spread everywhere. The screen showed very strange results. It could have been his fault because, trusting to the subtlety of the Buddhist light, he had employed the smallest cells. Should he have taken into account the fact that in the East the rational mind is augmented by "illumination"? Well, he told himself, the cells knew more than he did. On a molecular level, light cannot be disassociated from color, which is why shapes became visible in representation; whereas at the cellular level there was a disassociation,

and beyond what could be represented there was only "illumination" as a mental gesture. Small iridescent whirls appeared in
the space between the cells. The rivers of shadow flowed like
perpetually waving decorative streamers. He had gotten himself into a real mess. The optical readers were out of control.
What could the answer be? Maybe it was the colored concertinas hanging everywhere that were causing the distortion. The
concertinas could be giving off light. What if there were also
concertina cells? Perhaps without realizing it, he had made an
important scientific discovery ... No, he didn't think so. The
situation was still trivial.

IX

HE WAS ROUSED FROM THESE THOUGHTS BY JACQUE-
line calling to him. She was looking closely at one of the walls
of the shrine. He went over, accompanied by the little Buddhist monk, who had been standing silently by his side watching him at work. His wife pointed out a bronze plaque set in
the wall which had Korean writing on it. She wanted to know
what it said.

The little Buddhist monk translated it into French, but since
it was still largely incomprehensible, he had to explain that it
was a text in praise of a minister's widow.

How strange, commented Napoleon Chirac, that a translation should need a translation.

For her part, Jacqueline expressed her admiration at seeing someone reading so fluently — as their little friend had just
done — a text written in those fiendishly difficult Oriental ideograms. She said that she could spend her whole life studying
them without ever understanding a thing. (Although she did
like drawing them for her tapestries).

At this, they heard an amused laugh down at floor level. But at first, the short speech the little Buddhist monk embarked on was critical rather than amusing.

Oriental ideograms! he repeated scornfully. What a lack of discernment that innocent expression revealed. As if the Orient were a single exotic whole covering everything. It was no surprise that, if this was their starting point, Westerners needed not only translations of the translations, but translations of the translations of the translations and so on to infinity. And even so, he was afraid that infinity would not be enough for them to understand.

This was especially erroneous in the present instance, because as a matter of fact Korean writing was the simplest in the world. And it was so deliberately. The Korean alphabet, the hangeul, had been created in 1446 during the reign of Sejong during the Joseon dynasty. It had been given the name of Hunminjeongeum, in other words "The Correct Sounds for the Instruction of the People." Its promoter, the remarkable King Sejong, had ruled from 1418 to 1450. A great protector of learning, he regretted that his people did not have access to knowledge because of the difficulties of the Chinese characters that were used for writing. He therefore brought together all the scholars of his kingdom, and with their guidance this alphabet was created. At the proclamation of its launch he declared: "I have invented a series of twenty-eight letters that are very easy to learn, and it is my fervent desire that they serve to increase the happiness of my people."

Nowadays only twenty-four are used: fourteen consonants and ten vowels. It is a purely hieroglyphic system, which is extremely rare and possibly unique. The stroke representing each consonant imitates the position of the tongue needed to pronounce it. For example, the "g" is a small right angle, as in the top horizontal line and the right-hand vertical one in the depiction of a rectangle. A simple test suffices to demonstrate that this angle is a faithful representation of the position of the tongue as it pronounces the sound "g": that is, flat at the front, and then lower at the back. Or take the "n" sound. This is represented by a little angle that is the opposite of the "g"; in other words, it is the lower horizontal line and left-hand vertical of the same drawing of a rectangle.

As for the vowels, there are three basic ones. A horizontal line representing the earth, a vertical one representing a standing person, and a little circle representing the sky. (These are not hieroglyphs but mnemotechnic devices).

In writing, these signs are combined from the top, with a consonant and a vowel (and occasionally another consonant) forming a sound, in other words a syllable.

Children learn this alphabet at the age of two or three. Foreigners can get to grips with it in an hour or two, and thanks to its rational nature it is supremely easy to reproduce. Illiteracy is unknown in Korea. At first the alphabet was criticized precisely for being too easy. It was called Achingeul (morning letters) because they could in fact be learned in a morning, or Amgeul (women's letters).

This is the age-old conflict, still latent in Korea: knowledge for everyone, easy knowledge, as opposed to the Chinese ideograms; popular culture or high culture, television versus art.

What distinguishes Korea is that this conflict is found in distinct, opposing concepts of time, what could be seen as different "poetics" of time.

At this point the little Buddhist monk interrupted his explanations by saying that if they didn't believe him, they should try reading the text on the plaque. Why didn't they read it out loud? All they had to remember was that each sign indicated a position of the tongue and lips.

But they didn't know the language!

What did that matter? They should regard it not as a text but as an instruction manual, a kind of visual Braille.

They did as he suggested, hesitantly at first, then with greater confidence, and within seconds they were reading fluently. Napoleon Chirac realized that the relationship between the signs and the movements of his mouth were equivalent to that between the light and the flashing of the photoelectric cells when he looked at them on the screen.

Jacqueline commented that she now understood the meaning of the text on the plaque. Her husband agreed: it was the same for him. They could see what a vast difference there was between translation and direct reading. It seemed undeniable that translations were no use at all.

One moment though: how could they possibly understand it, when they didn't know Korean? They had only learned the alphabet, not the language. Were they the same thing?

"I told you it was easy. When something is easy, it is completely easy. But no one believes it. Not even the proof convinces them."

X

THE TEMPLE'S EMPTINESS HAD GRADUALLY BEEN FILL-
ing up. From the moment they arrived monks had been discreetly filing in and wandering around absorbed in their arcane
duties or prayers. They drew no attention to themselves, and appeared not to pay any to the strangers. This however was a false
impression, and when the French couple did look at them more
closely, they could tell that they were fascinated by the photographer's work and that it was only their timidity which, fortunately, prevented them from approaching the camera, touching it, and wanting to look through the viewfinder, like savages.
They restricted their curiosity to sideways glances and to re-
peatedly passing by, pretending to be doing things they were not
really doing. After each approach, they hid so that they could
continue to watch from a distance, but they must have had little
practice at hiding, because they did it ridiculously badly, thinking that a trunk of only four inches in diameter, or a stone eight
inches high was enough to conceal them. Far from discourag-
ing them, the laughter this produced in the French couple only
stimulated them to show their interest more openly, which they
did with enchanting smiles and slight bows.

Soon afterward there was a consultation and all the monks withdrew to one of the buildings, only to reappear a short time later carrying bags, bottles and tablecloths. The little Buddhist monk told the French pair they were being invited to a picnic.

They accepted, although Napoleon Chirac insisted it could not be a very long one, as his work was pressing. A chorus of agreement and more bows: they would never allow themselves to interfere in the work of such a distinguished guest: far from it! And it really was far from it because, rather than being pressing, time adapted to all the interruptions.

They had already laid out the cloths on the floor of the shrine and spread different-sized bowls, glasses and chopsticks on them. They all sat down. The French couple were not altogether surprised to see that all the dishes were plastic, and that the potato chips and candies were from supermarket packages. The only drink was Coca-Cola.

After the first few mouthfuls, Napoleon Chirac felt obliged to give a brief explanation of his intentions and way of working. This produced a wave of polite smiles, and more brief bows. It did not matter whether they had understood or not, because they agreed with everything anyway.

Attracted by the smell of food (if this industrially produced food had a smell) a big black dog came over. The monks greeted her enthusiastically, stroking her and offering her handfuls of nibbles and sweets which the dog devoured with great delight.

"Aren't they bad for her?"

"She's used to it."

They filled a bowl with Coca-Cola, and the dog licked it up in seconds, curling and uncurling a huge yellow tongue.

"What an unnatural color for a tongue!"

"They dye it."

The unnatural qualities of Firefly (that was the dog's name) went far beyond this. The temple's sacred pet, she displayed elements of shamanism latent in the sophisticated northern Buddhism. The monks left her to roam freely, and she took full advantage of this because she was both inquisitive and sociable. She always came back, however; and indeed, she was always present, as she had demonstrated on this occasion. To avoid problems, once she had had her first litter (five puppies, which had been distributed among the region's faithful) they had taken her to a reputable animal clinic to be neutered. It was a routine operation, in this case carried out without problems. The next day, Firefly returned to the temple and to her roaming. Imagine then the monks' surprise when they saw that male dogs still pursued her as before, and with the same intentions. When they went to the clinic to complain, the vets were as intrigued as they were, and carried out a close examination. No: the operation had been a success; it was impossible for the bitch to be still attracting males because the organs producing the necessary smell had been removed. They even took X-rays to see if by some extraordinary chance Firefly had a second set of glands that had escaped their scalpel. Of course, this was not the case. After the monks' third or fourth visit, one of the vets came to the temple, where he was able to see that the chasing and hounding continued. They gave up, and that was the end of it. The only explanation they could offer was that it must be a "psychological" case, even though that did not make much sense.

Napoleon Chirac nodded thoughtfully. He said he knew exactly what it was like. Something similar had happened to him many years earlier, when he made his living from taking portraits before he devoted himself to art photography. One lady of whom he had to make a semiofficial portrait (she was the lover of his country's president) had insisted on dabbing on perfume before their session, because she said this completely changed the nature of her image. He had dismissed this as either superstition or mania, but was still sufficiently curious to carry out the experiment, and as a result had to admit that she was right.

The same was true of sounds, he added. The ones coming from the speakers at that moment would doubtless modify the images the camera would capture. If he had time, he would take two series of photographs, one with music and the other without, to show them the difference. If that is, he added, his kind hosts would agree to switch off the sound system for a while.

He had suggested this out of politeness, in order to make plausible a bargain that he had no intention of honoring. To his surprise, the monks took this very seriously. After glancing at one another to consider it, they replied that no, they did not agree to turn off the music even for a moment. This was accompanied by their constant smiles and bows, repeated on all sides, but their refusal was so categorical and unexpected that the photographer's face must have betrayed his dismay, and so they condescended to offer him an explanation. This was even more un-expected: without music, the temple was too depressing...

How frivolous they were. The presence of music could not have any ritual function because it was made up of the most vulgar "top-ten" radio hits for teenagers; and if they found the temple depressing, why had they become monks? They didn't seem like real Buddhist monks, or at least not like the conventional image a foreigner might have of their kind. The truth is there is no reason that a foreigner's conventional idea or prejudice should coincide with reality, and in general it doesn't. During their first day in Korea they had been able to correct some of their misapprehensions, but the little Buddhist monk who was their guide was too small a sample for them to make any sweeping generalizations.

The best way out of this awkward moment was to change topics. The French couple did this, although not completely: they simply went back to the dog, which was still with them. Was she a guard dog? No. There was nothing to guard. But she was very helpful. She pulled the little cart the monks used to go for trips in around the park. It was so big, and its most delightful spots were so far away, that they would never reach them without the aid of Firefly.

How was this possible? Even though the dog was large, she was not enormous. And the monks were not that diminutive. Another enigma yet to be resolved.

XI

IT WAS TRUE THAT THEY WERE OF NORMAL SIZE, BUT
only on the outside; mentally they were like children. They
demonstrated this when Napoleon Chirac went back to work,
and they started their jokes. Or perhaps they weren't jokes? A
cosmopolitan traveler, the Frenchman knew that "jokes" could
easily lead to misunderstandings. If assumptions were different,
the humorous could seem serious, and the serious be taken as
another token of humor. Often, the lack of understanding between civilizations was nothing more than a gap in the appre-
ciation of a joke. And this mismatch had survived globalization,
which nowadays had converted all civilizations into one. What
had replaced extinct exoticism within this unified culture were
differences of level: between children and adults, for example,
or between low and high culture. However, everything seemed
to indicate that these alternatives were one and the same thing,
with children, the popular and the humorous on one side, and
on the other, the adult, learned and serious.

Looking around him at the monks, Napoleon Chirac wondered about the future of his work. Even if they didn't wager

exclusively on posterity, artists always counted on some kind of historical prolongation. But in the period of history into which he had been born, everything tended toward the ephemeral. Fed on television, the new generations were not storing up time, without which art did not exist. His photos would need many years to "mature" and be surrounded by the aura of a lost world which makes a work valuable. And by that time, if things continued in the same direction, the public's taste would have fatally degenerated.

And yet, returning to work after the picnic and before he became aware of the monks' antics, he had felt a frisson of euphoria when he thought of the fleeting nature of light. This was a contradiction, although possibly it made sense in the place where he found himself. Here in Korea, the eternal was produced thanks to what was fleeting, and not in spite of it. And the paradox did not end there ...

This wasn't the first time that his reflections on the artistic process had become impossible to communicate, like a vertiginous spiral of silence (or unformulated thoughts). He was left alone, and in his case this meant being separated mentally from his wife. The vertigo inspired by the emptiness of these moments was due to the fact that his marriage was the real story of his life. And the marriage was gradually turning into a dry husk where it was only possible to follow the fossilized remains of the tentacles of the paradox. Paradoxical tentacles. In his youth, he had loved the beautiful Jacqueline Bloodymary madly, when she was a bacteriologist psychically in thrall to the sinister director of her laboratory. After the liberation, they had both chosen the path of art, but it could be said that they had done so from the opposite shores of time: him in the instant of the click of a camera shutter; she in the months if not years that it took weavers to complete a tapestry. And yet, for him to reach that click required a great deal of work with space and time, whereas for her, to reach that slow task of weaving she needed only the instant of finding the idea. This contradiction kept them apart. Now as he watched her strolling happily, filled with inspiration among the flowers and birds, he was drowning in a sea of doubts.

Buddhism was becoming increasingly devalued for him. At first he couldn't believe it, but now he had to accept the evidence: the monks were playing jokes on him. They must have understood that his intention was to photograph the circle of the temple empty of people, and were sabotaging his efforts by walking in front of the camera. They didn't do this out of spite, but because they were so childish. And they did it just like small children, pretending not to in a way that fooled no one. Giggling, whispering, glancing at him, and making throwaway theatrical gestures whenever he looked at them. Two or three of them would link arms and walk directly in front of the camera, holding back their laughter only for it to burst out moments later when they ran behind a tree to watch the following group's trick or to prepare their own next one. They perfected their maneuvers with fake excuses, calling to each other from one side to the other, or pretending (clumsily) they had something urgent to tell a colleague, or that they had forgotten something and had to cross again where they had just crossed. Or they sent Firefly: that really amused them. They would throw a stick for her to retrieve, or call her to give her a pat that could not be postponed.

Napoleon Chirac let them get on with it. At first it amused him, but in the end their puerile persistence annoyed him. He did not think the photographs would suffer, because he was keeping the shutter open to take long exposures, so that nothing that moved would be registered. But there was something else, which led him to think they must know more about photography than he had first thought. This shouldn't have astonished him, if many tourists visited the temple. He noticed that their movements as they passed through the field covered by the lens were not regular. They slowed down at particular points which were always the same, although different for each monk. Not only did they slow down: there was a point at which they came to a halt, before which they changed gesture and posture, only to resume the normal ones immediately afterward and continue on their way, accelerating imperceptibly until they left the circle. This was done so quickly that he was never sure he had seen anything. But it was repeated after a few minutes by the same people in exactly the same spot. Were they pulling a face, or making a comic gesture? If they repeated it sufficiently frequently and were careful enough to do so in exactly the same spot (a millimetric mistake would ruin the effect) in the end they would leave an impression on the photographic film and the image would be full of monks fixed by the same mechanism that should have rendered them invisible. A triumph of coordination, possible only thanks to that kind of inhuman lifelong training in which the Orient specialized. But what a gratuitous, useless triumph! All it could do was to transform movement into immobility, the invisible into the visible, a joke about motion into a joke about seeing. And Firefly had obviously also been trained.

Since the tripod gyrated on its own, Napoleon Chirac had nothing to do, and so fell into a musing that expanded on these recent reflections. To him it seemed as though destiny might also be fixing in grotesque grimaces a life lived at a speed that no emulsion (God's ever-open eye) could capture. And all thanks to small, pointless repetitions.

He felt that his art was fragile, that he himself was fragile, and became so panic-stricken that all these thoughts were driven from his mind.

How often did he have to tell himself that it was better to enjoy the moment and forget his worries? To distance himself and lose himself in what was there, which was substantially more than an instant: a sublime afternoon suspended from the trees, the chirping of the birds, the depths of the stilled breeze. But this was easier to say than do. His anxiety was linked precisely to the instant: that is where it emerged from and where it returned.

The concertina lanterns with their painfully bright colors continued to be revealed in the photo, continued to "appear," while he tried to think and feel and live in time.

XII

IN THE MEANTIME, JACQUELINE BLOODYMARY HAD wandered off along the paths in the park. She was used to disappearing when she accompanied her husband on his photographic excursions (and he always insisted she accompany him), because since the images traveled through three hundred and sixty degrees, there was no place for her. This was how she had ended up with a better knowledge than his of the countries they visited, and had built up a store of sights and anecdotes that enriched her conversation on their return. In her mind, it had also come to symbolize the role of women: "there was no place for her" in a man's work, even if this work encompassed the entire horizon, or because it did.

Faithful to his strategy of cultivating the wives, the little Buddhist monk followed her. He surmised that she wanted to talk; he had noticed she had been affected by the story of Firefly. As she had listened, an air of deep sadness shrouded her features, where until then a smiling, polite calm had predominated.

He found her sitting on a stone bench behind a small mound. She had been crying, and her tears had dried. With gentlemanly tact, without intruding, he talked about the weather, about the vegetation surrounding them, occasionally slipping in an allusion to the melancholy mood of the time and place, in order to suggest the reason for, without explicitly mentioning it, a depressed state of mind. With a similar intention he sighed now and then, but this sounded strange in such a small person; sighs are things giants do, not dwarves; elephants, not microbes. He said that the colored lanterns adorning the park were the "automata of sighs."

She was not really paying him any attention. She agreed absentmindedly, and continued to stare off into the distance.

"I'm disturbing you. You prefer to be alone with your thoughts. I'll leave you and go for a stroll."

"No, no," replied Jacqueline, coming out of her reverie. "Please stay. In fact, I need to talk."

And after a sigh which, given her size, sounded more natural, she asked rhetorically, What woman did not need to talk? Wives were traditionally accused of talking too much, but that was unfair. There were so many silences that accumulated in the life of a married woman, so many unspoken words pressing down on the membranes of sleeplessness … In the end, it was like not existing.

But, her diminutive interlocutor insisted, there were other forms of expression. Life itself was expression. And in the case of an artist like herself …

No! There was no substitute for the proper articulation of

language. What was not said with words in well-turned phrases was not said at all. And even when she cherished the hope that her modest, subordinate artistic endeavor might say something, her husband had been sure to silence her. Why otherwise had he chosen this circular format for his photographs, which encompassed everything and left her stuck in a center that no one could reach, like one of those spellbound princesses in fairy tales?

She must have anticipated some expression of doubt from the little Buddhist monk because she immediately added that she was putting far too poetic a gloss on a more sordid and much crueler reality. In real life there were no enchanted princesses, only hopes extinguished by routine, by prosaic and gradual deaths. Her marriage now was nothing more than an empty shell. She had no idea why they dragged around the world a fiction that weighed on them like a curse. Out of inertia, convenience, fear? She felt she was wasting the last shreds of her youth next to a man she did not love; a selfish, unhealthy man obsessed with his stupid photographic tricks. If at least he were a true artist! But not even then: she had no vocation for self-sacrifice. She wanted to be herself, whatever that was worth.

But couldn't they rebuild ... ?

There was nothing to rebuild. There had never been anything. She regretted that she had become this ultraconventional figure of the wife who once she starts complaining about her husband cannot stop until she has reached the heights of nihilism,

but it was true: there had never been love, or spiritual commu-
nion, not even good sex. Can you believe, she asked him, that in
my whole life I've never had an orgasm?

Somewhat embarrassed, the little Buddhist monk admitted
he could believe it.

The story of the black bitch Firefly had affected her through
a kind of interspecies recognition. Especially because, above
and beyond the easy equivalences, she herself had become the
subject of a story that could be told in a drawing room or a
monks' picnic and give rise to sympathetic or mocking comments … and then be forgotten. There was nothing memorable
about the novel of her life, which anyway she had not written.
Who said that truths could be told through art? That was absurd. What was needed was to learn to talk, and to do it well.
The stuff of language was not subordinate to feelings or "expression"; on the contrary, it was primordial: everything began and ended there. It was like jokes. Let him try telling a joke
through tapestries.

"But not all jokes are linguistic."

"The good ones are."

What was she doing talking to him about jokes, after the
lesson he had given them on the subject? Perhaps for her, he
said, the time for jokes had already come and gone; perhaps it
would be better to give in to tiredness, to disgust, and forget everything, even her resentment. But it was inevitable that some
jokes would remain in suspense, waiting for the punch line
(because, since she was not Korean, she put this at the end).

Although possibly he should not talk of resignation, or even of acceptance. Reality could do without those gestures, which were mere psychobabble. The biological process was not like traditional Korean jokes; weariness and old age came at the end, not the beginning. It was like the career of those artists who as they approach the finish begin to lose energy and inventiveness, and start doing things in a slapdash way, however they can. After all, a joke that goes on too long is also bound to have a hasty, untidy ending.

XIII

BY THE TIME A SHORT SHARP WHISTLE INDICATED THAT the camera's automatic mechanisms were completing their 360-degree sweep, the "blue hour" had arrived in the sky. An intense, deep luminosity filled the air. The birds had fallen silent; the monks gone off to sleep. This moment, which prolonged itself, was day and night at the same time. A radiant night and a dark day. In the depths of the sanctuary, the fat, bronze Buddha still glowed. Hanging from the edge of the shrine, a drop of Coca-Cola refused to fall, held by its own transparent brilliance, streaked with veins of gold and fiery red, its liquid curves reflecting the near and the far.

Napoleon and Jacqueline dismantled the tripod and picked up the photoelectric cells, wrapped the rolls of negatives in black plush and put everything into their backpack. They commented on the session and anticipated a satisfactory outcome.

"But what's become of our little friend?"

The distraction of packing up had led them to lose sight of the little Buddhist monk. They looked for him at their feet, among the columns of the balcony, behind the geraniums under the mushrooms. For a moment they feared they had unwittingly stuffed him in their backpack along with everything else. Eventually, when they looked up, they spotted him in the distance, doing gymnastics on top of a mound. His tiny figure stood out alone, dark but with every detail of his silhouette visible and clear and, whether due to the distance, the undulating terrain or the dim light, it took on a strange monumentality. It might also have been because of the activity he was engaged in. It was plain he was a practiced gymnast because of the harmonious precision with which he carried out his routine of bends, stretches and twists. He must do this every day, but today he had not had the opportunity until now. They stood fascinated as they gazed at him, thinking: "How strange he is!" Above all, the colors made the scene unreal. How strange it was ... Napoleon Chirac attempted to analyze the elements that made up the strangeness of the situation; he realized that throughout the day, caught up in the constant succession of events, he had not thought seriously about what was going on. He had an analytical mind of which he was generally very proud, except for when he forgot to use it. Now, taking advantage of this interval of calm, he set it in motion. Out of a sense of professional respect, the first element he isolated was the light. He had not found any complaint with the light all day, and the vigorous phantom of it that still persisted could have provided a thousand photographers with a living. It was truly sublime, or perfect, or any other laudatory adjective that might be used for this homogenous glow descending from a homogeneously blue sky, a blue as dark and shiny as a topaz. This admiration for the blue hour that had inspired so many poets and painters had a long history in his own life. He had been privileged to admire it in all latitudes, and it was always the same, although of course he had never seen it illuminate a tiny little man doing gymnastics on a distant hill. A small animated idol who threw no shadow on the ground ... This last point, which proved to be the key to the enigma, was logical, because the blue hour occurs when the sun has completely set and in the sky there are not even clouds to reflect or concentrate its rays from the far side of the horizon.

The key was hovering close to his awareness, and at that moment crossed the threshold and left him dumbfounded: there had never been a sun in the sky! Throughout their long day of adventures, the sun had been absent. It hadn't been hidden behind clouds or mists: from the morning on, the sky had been clear and bright, the air as sparkling as a diamond.

He told this to Jacqueline in such an anxious rush that at first she did not understand. He had to repeat himself.

Are you sure, Nap?

Fickle as only a woman can be, she had forgotten her resentment and relapsed into the friendly complicity of their years of marriage.

Absolutely sure. I'm never wrong about that kind of thing.

Yes ... I was thinking something strange was going on.

They whispered together excitedly, not once taking their eyes off the little Buddhist monk.

Why then, she went on, did I feel so hot at times?

At times? So had he! But at others he had been freezing. So had she! Neither of them had mentioned it, in order not to interrupt the flow of conversation that had in fact never been interrupted. The revelations all fell into place. The sun was a tiny glandular nerve center situated in the rear half of the brain, where it regulated body temperature; without it, the waves of heat and cold switched back and forth at random …

One thing led to another, and their suspicions grew and grew. The little Buddhist monk had led them into a parallel world they had to escape from before it was too late. But how? They didn't think they would be able to find the train station to take them back to the city center. They had been very rash in allowing themselves to be taken so far, but before that they had been even more rash in trusting everything they were seeing and hearing uncritically, without thinking … At that moment, a big black limousine with a French Embassy license plate pulled up behind them. They had been so involved in their discussion they had not heard it, and anyway its engine produced no more than a scarcely audible purr. It had tinted windows. The back door opened and an urgent voice told them to get in. They did so, not forgetting their things.

The deus ex machina who made room for them on the back seat was an extremely elegant and perfumed Frenchman. He immediately ordered the chauffeur to drive off, and then began recriminating with them (as they had done with themselves) for having come so far; it had cost him a lot of hard work to find them. The excused themselves by saying they were not the ones to blame: their guide ... Your guide! The Frenchman interrupted them scornfully: Great little guide! The implicit joke in the double meaning of that word "little" led to a lessening of the tension. Napoleon and Jacqueline both giggled, and suddenly realized they had been repressing the desire to laugh since that morning. Jean-Claude de la Chaumière, Minister of Culture and Interfaith Affairs, introduced himself suavely, but with a hint of impatience. It was lucky they had telephoned the consulate before leaving the hotel. They asked how he had managed to find them. Luck, chance, a hunch. The car interior was padded and at a warm, even temperature. The chauffeur wore a red plastic cap and was concentrating on his driving. They were speeding along the narrow park paths, sweeping off the leaves on the peonies that lined the route. The diplomat pressed the tip of his finger against the car window to point something out. The little Buddhist monk was chasing after them through the trees as fast as he could, waving his arms and shouting inaudible words. He did not catch them, and they were soon on the highway, still picking up speed.

Can you explain, Monsieur de la Chaumière, who that little creature was?

Of course he could, said their savior. Nothing easier, especially since he had already been obliged to explain it more than once. To start with, the little Buddhist monk was not a human being like them, but a 3-D digital creation. That was so obvious he couldn't understand how they had not realized, although they shouldn't feel too bad about it because they were not the first to be fooled. Like others before them, they had the excuse of having just arrived, desperate for exoticism, credulous and blinded by the illusions of the myth of Korea. Let this be a lesson to them; now they had been warned, the next time they should be more observant. After all, it was not so hard to spot, because the fake was obvious: first and foremost because of his tiny size, which they must have noticed. And if that were not enough, there was something obviously unfinished about him, because he was only a prototype. Because of contractual and commercial problems, they had broken off their work when it was only half completed. Since he was only a "rough draft," an unpolished version, the creature showed clear traces of the manufacturing process. You had to be either very unobservant or very accommodating not to see this.

The photographer and his wife confessed shamefacedly that they had accepted everything far too easily. How innocent they had been! There was no excuse. But why had he chosen them as victims?

By chance. It could have been anybody else, provided they were European or North American. Foreigners were programmed in the character's memory chip, and this was related to the contractual difficulties he had mentioned. The creators of the Show of the Little Buddhist Monk had thought of it as something they could export in order for it to be economically viable. When they were halfway through their work, they learned of the customs barriers the western countries were raising, under pressure from TV companies and the big studios. And so they postponed finishing their project until they could discover some loophole to take advantage of. They were using their pilot model to do this. That was why he was allowed to roam freely, in search of unwary victims. Fortunately, all the consular services had been warned, so that they could act rapidly and things never became too serious.

XIV

NIGHT HAD FALLEN, AND THE LITTLE BUDDHIST MONK had been left all alone, far from home. His plan had failed: the birds had flown. With hindsight, he realized he had let his imagination run away with him. How was someone so small and weak going to trap such huge, powerful quarry in his nets? Greater feats had been heard of, but not in cruel reality.

The effort had also taken it out of him. He felt completely exhausted from all the day's tension. He had not been able to take his siestas (because normally he had three, one in mid-morning, one after lunch, and the third before supper); he had been on the move the whole time; and in addition, being constantly in company was tiring for him, as he could only relax when he was on his own. Now that this much needed solitude had arrived, he could not enjoy it because he had gone beyond his limits and every nerve in his body was as taut as a steel cable. The lax muscles could no longer support the weight of this metallic structure. He was weary to the point of collapse, and believed he could no longer stay upright ...

And yet ... Not only did he have to stay upright, but he had to walk and even run. He had to make one last huge effort, one that made it impossible for him to think of resting. The collapse of his strategy in getting close to the foreigners and the consequent pain of failure was no more than a little added anxiety compared to the emergency he still had to face: getting home.

And getting there quickly! There wasn't a second to lose. Time was taking its revenge. All the magical suspensions of the moment that he had used to enchant the French couple were dissolving, leaving only an inflexible, unavoidable horizon.

Between him and home lay a forest that he had to cross on foot. He was not afraid of getting lost (fear did not even enter his mind) because he knew it from memory and could not get lost if he wanted to, even in complete darkness, as it would doubtless be on this occasion. But darkness was never complete for him, because his own body, or possibly its movement, gave off a glow. In reality he was not thinking of the forest or the darkness: his thoughts were limited with absolute insistence to the goal of his journey: his home. He might have said—and would have done had there been anyone to talk to—"My home is my castle." And his home was pure light. The correct term would have been "little home" because of how small and empty it was. In his home there was literally nothing, apart from a television set that was always on at night.

It was the light from that screen, intensified by his sense of urgency, that was guiding him, just as the shooting star had guided the shepherds of myth. In his troubled imagination it became pure light, an endless, saving regard. In fact it was the television that was the reason for his urgency. At ten o'clock sharp, the moment after the end of Children's Scheduling was signaled and some cute little dolls packed the children off to bed with a lullaby, a program he could not miss was due to begin. He had been waiting weeks for it, and that very morning when he went out it had been uppermost in his mind, to the extent that, even though it was only nine o'clock, he told himself he would just go out for a walk and get a bit of fresh air and then come back quickly so that he would not miss a minute of the program ... However, the adventure with the French couple had intervened, and now he was in this dreadful hurry. He could not believe his bad luck, although he had to, because it was his own fault: he had been too reckless, and had allowed improvisation to take over.

Well, no use crying over spilt milk. He didn't waste time lamenting, or allow self-recrimination to paralyze him. He was already in the forest, frantically moving his tiny legs along what he hoped was the straightest line. He knew that "a thousand-league journey starts with one step," and was taking all the steps he could. He weaved in and out of the trees, skirted bushes, searched for firm support on the roots jutting above ground to launch himself forward, always forward. He stumbled and fell, and sometimes rolled over, but nothing could stop him. His one thought was to arrive, to get there in time.

He couldn't even calculate whether he would arrive, because he had no idea how long it took to cross the forest. Although he had often done so, he had never timed himself. Besides, he had no idea what time it was. He did have a wristwatch, but could not see it in the darkness. He tried, raising his arm almost up to his face and attempting to make sure the feeble glow he gave off lit the minuscule dial, but he couldn't see a thing, and didn't want to waste any more time. So he lowered his arm and set off even more rapidly than before. A little further on, and his curiosity got the better of him. He attempted a second time to make out the position of the watch hands. It seemed to him there was only one ... were they on top of each other, making it ten to ten? But then he thought he could see three hands, or twelve, or none at all. The only thing he could be certain of was that time kept passing inexorably by, and it would soon be ten o'clock, if it wasn't that already. And he was filled with a boundless anxiety at the thought that he might miss the program, or worse still, that he was missing it at that very moment, because they weren't going to wait for him to show it, at ten ... ten o' clock sharp ...

It wasn't just another program; he had reason to consider it so important. It had been previewed for weeks, and from the moment he heard about it, along with many millions more Koreans, he had been on tenterhooks, waiting for the date and time of its transmission.

The program involved an incredible novelty, the result of recent advances in design and animation technology. The happy combination of a team of doctors, artists and computer whiz kids had succeeded in creating a model of the female sexual organs. For the first time in history, this had allowed the exact location of the clitoris to be identified. It was not that the existence of this tiny pleasure spot or its position had been unknown, but the man in the street, the average husband or lover, still had difficulties finding it. This was due to the confusion produced by verbal descriptions of it, a confusion never resolved by the drawings in books illustrating these descriptions. On the contrary: it was the drawings that had ended up making the difficulty impenetrable. The two-dimensional representations had all the well-known limitations, but these became insurmountable when it came to the complex "empty volumes" of the external area of the female reproductive organ. It did not help that humans had evolved from standing on four legs to becoming bipeds, which meant these volumes were in a position that conventional drawings could not properly depict.

The solid, three-dimensional models that pedagogical ingenuity had come up with, besides being hidden in university lecture theaters or anatomical museums, had been too small and hard to manipulate to fulfil their function ... Until now, nobody had imagined that the ideal medium for bringing the Good News to the public was television. The 3-D animation, digitalized and driven by a specially developed program, instantly resolved all the problems of comprehension. TV viewers could take a virtual stroll through this first interior, or "exterior interior," with all its nooks and crannies, its superimposed concavities and convexities. By identifying with the eye of the camera, they could finally orient themselves and discover once and for all where this elusive little phantom was to be found. And the Korean people were to have the privilege of being the first to know.

Conscious of the importance of sexual pleasure in life, the

little Buddhist monk had waited impatiently for the transmission. The contemporary passion for television had finally found an object worthy of the eagerness with which a program was anticipated. Recalling his own expectation was like being wounded by an arrow of time in the depths of the dark night, and made him even more anxious. There was no way he could miss it! To him it was a life-or-death affair, and he refused to consider whether he was behaving like a child. Wasn't this on the contrary the most adult thing that had ever happened in his life? And there was no question of waiting for the repeat, because there wouldn't be one. The producer had been through a lot just to get permission for this screening. The legal battle had lasted for months, and even now had not been finally resolved: the transmission was going ahead thanks to an injunction that could still be appealed, as a defiant gesture of "now or never." The next day, the Korean newspapers would be full of indignant readers' letters from the usual reactionaries, and the scandal would put so much pressure on the judges that it would be banned forever. Besides, nobody would call for it to be repeated. Why would they, if they had already discovered what they were after? A predictable psychological reaction could come into play: those who already knew the secret (the path to the hidden object) would not want the others to discover it. It did not matter that tens of millions of viewers would have seen the program; the unique quality of the occasion made the revelation invaluable. They would rub their hands gleefully, telling themselves "anyone who missed it has missed it forever." They would be able to gloat at their superiority over these real or virtual losers. And the losers could well be real, as perfectly real as he himself would be if he did not arrive in time.

Had he reached the center of the forest? He had no way of knowing. All of a sudden he couldn't recognize his surroundings, even if all along he couldn't see a thing. The screen of trees was so thick it seemed almost solid; he groped his way along, rushing up and down on the uneven ground, squeezing his way between two trunks or falling headlong into a bush and kicking out desperately until he freed himself from the suffocating clutch of flowers that were as cold and silky as fish.

Looking up, he could see the topmost foliage as black on black, being whipped around by a wind that did not reach the ground. Turning his head, he could make out the yellowish wake he himself had left behind. He was no longer looking where he put his feet, while at the same time he was paying ever more attention to it. He saw that the ground was rising and remembered, with a sigh of dismay, that there were mountains in the middle of the forest, and that he would have to cross them as well. Mountains that were part of the forest, hidden beneath the trees but still high enough to have ravines, rivers, snowy peaks and dangerous bridges suspended over abysses.

He did not slow down. He would not have done so even if he had remembered there was also an ocean in his way. On the contrary, he tried to go faster, but had reached such an extreme state of exhaustion that his legs no longer obeyed him. They were like rubber. The tears of despair coursing down his cheeks were no fuel for his flagging machine. But even in the depths of his paralysis he was still confident of arriving. Of course, the depths were not the surface, and here he was aware of the unassailable distance between the size of the forest and his own small stature. However many times he multiplied his tiny footsteps, they were pathetic millimeters. If only he were not so weary ...

In one final spasm of hope, he told himself that the subjective component of time might be deceiving him. There were occasions when mental tension, or simple impatience, made what was in fact a minute seem like an hour. Unfortunately this was not the case now. What he was seeing was the evolution of species, and that took more than a minute.

This was not a metaphor: he was really seeing. The faint glow he left in his wake had spread all around him, and the darkness yielded to the dim outlines of a gothic, overloaded nature, which from his point of view looked monumental. The trees were monsters draped in moss and creepers, the flowers opened and closed, nocturnal wasps the size of doves climbed the spiraling shadows; rabbits bigger than he was peeped out of their holes to look at him. His panting sounded fearful beside the hooting of owls. His progress became increasingly difficult on the slippery wetness of the soft slopes. And yet he carried on, his chest crushed by the weight of anguish, and in his desire to reach home in time he no longer walked but ran, or tried to run, deep in those unmoving valleys, while the forest continued to cast on him its vast, dark distances.

MARCH 25, 2005

THE PROOF

"WANNAFUCK?"

Marcia was so startled she didn't understand the question. She looked hastily around to see where it came from ... Although it wasn't so out of place—perhaps nothing else was to be expected—here in this labyrinth of voices and glances that were both transparent, light, inconsequential and yet at the same time dense, rapid, slightly wild. But if you went around expecting something ...

Three blocks before Plaza Flores on this side of the avenue, an adolescent world came into its own. Stationary but mobile, three-dimensional, it defined its own boundaries, the volume it created. There were big groups of boys and girls—more of the former—gathered in the doorways of the two record shops, the empty area around Cine Flores that stood between them, and clustered against the parked cars. At this time of day they were all out of school and met up here. She had also left school two hours earlier (she was in her fourth year), but was a long way away, fifteen blocks further down, in Caballito. She was out for her daily walk. Marcia was overweight and had a back problem that wasn't serious at the age of sixteen, but could become so in the future. No one had recommended that she walk; she did it out of a therapeutic instinct. For other reasons as well, above all habit; the serious depression she had suffered, which had reached its climax a few months earlier, meant that to survive she had been constantly on the move, and now she did it just because, out of inertia or superstition. By this stage of her exercise, when she was already close to the point of turning back, it was as though she were slowing down; penetrating this new, adolescent space after the more or less neutral stretch along Avenida Rivadavia that separated the two districts meant she was going increasingly slower, even though she did not slacken her pace.

She came up against floating signs; every step, every swing of her arms met endless responses and allusions ... with its sprawling adolescent world, arriving in Flores was like raising a mirror to her own story, only slightly distant from its original location—not far, easily reachable on an evening walk. It was only logical that time should become denser when she got there. Outside her story she felt she was gliding along too rapidly, like a body in the ether where there was no resistance. Nor should there be too much resistance or she would be paralyzed, as had happened to her during the rather tragic period of her life that was already vanishing into the past.

Although it was only seven o'clock, it had already grown dark. It was winter, and night fell early. Not dark night; that would come later. In the direction she was walking, Marcia had the sunset in front of her; at the far end of the avenue there was an intense red, violet and orangey glow she could only see as she drew closer to Flores and Rivadavia made a gentle bend. It was still almost daytime when she set out, but the light faded quickly; in midwinter it would have been dark by half past six, but the season had moved on and these were no longer what you could call the shortest days of the year, although it was still cold, twilight descended quickly, and nightfall was already in the air when school was out at five. There must still have been light in the atmosphere, even at seven o'clock, but the street was so brightly lit that the sky looked dark by comparison. Especially when she reached the more commercial part of Flores, near the square, with the illuminated shop windows and canopies. This made the red glow of the sunset in the distance seem incongruous, although it was no longer red, more like a weak blue shadow with gray streaks around it. Here the brightness of the mercury lights was dazzling, perhaps because of the crowd of young people who were looking at each other and talking, waiting or arguing loudly. In the previous blocks where there were fewer people (it was very cold, and those who weren't young, with their ridiculous need to meet their friends, preferred to stay indoors) the lights appeared less bright; although it was true it had been earlier in the evening when she passed them by. Time seemed to be going backward, from an unknown midnight, toward evening, toward day.

She didn't feel it, or shouldn't have felt it, because she herself was part of the system, but all those young people were wasting their time. The system meant being happy. That was what it was all about, and Marcia understood that perfectly, even though she couldn't be part of it. Or thought she couldn't. However that might have been, she entered an enchanted realm, which was not in any particular spot, but was rather a fortuitous moment of the evening. Had she reached it? Or had it reached her? Had it been waiting for her? She didn't ask herself any more questions, because she was already there. She had forgotten she was walking, that she was going in a certain direction (she wasn't headed anywhere anyway) through the soft resistance of the light and darkness, silence, and the looks exchanged between face and face.

They looked at each other, met one another: that was why they were out on the street. They talked, shouted, whispered secrets among themselves, but everything quickly dissolved into nothing. That was the joy of finding oneself in a particular place and moment. Marcia had to sidestep to avoid groups inside which a secret was circulating. The secret was being young or not. Even so, she couldn't help looking, seeing, pay more attention. Boys and girls were constantly peeling off from the little groups, scurrying this way and that, in the end always returning, talking, gesticulating. They filled this entire stretch of the avenue; they seemed to be constantly coming and going, but the number remained the same. They gave an impression of shifting sociability. In fact, it was as if they weren't stationary, but were just passing through, exactly as she was. It wasn't a place of resistance, except a poetic, imaginary one, but a gentle tumult of loud and soft laughter. They all seemed to be arguing. Asshole! Asshole! was the most common insult, although nobody ever came to blows. They accused each other of all sorts of things, but that was just their way. They did not watch her go by; they weren't silent or immobile enough for that. Besides, it was only an instant, a few feet. She walked on, crossing Calle Gavilán, where she hit the real crowds. This side of the intersection, where the huge Duncan café stood, was darker. There seemed to be a lot more people here. Now they were typical kids from Flores: long hair, leather jackets, motorbikes parked on the sidewalk. A latent urgency hung in the air. There was a closed newspaper stand, with a florist's next to it; there were small knots of teens for a further twenty or thirty feet, right up to the first entrance of the shopping mall; it was outside the record shop there that the number of youngsters displaying themselves reached its height, for the moment at least. Marcia knew that on the next corner, opposite a pharmacy, at this time of evening there was always a gaggle of kids. She was venturing into the most typical part of the neighborhood. For now, though, she was still on the corner, where the Duncan café was, packed with bikers ... Marcia could already hear music from the record shop: The Cure, which she loved.

The music changed her mood, took her to its silent conclusion. Since this had not happened with the music from the two earlier record shops, it must have been due to how good it was, although possibly it was the climax of an accumulation of impressions. The music was the remaining resistance needed to make the mall completely fluid. Every look, every voice she slipped past mingled with the night. Because it was night. The day was over and night was in the world; at this hour in summer it was still broad daylight; but now it was night. Not the kind of night for sleeping, the real one, but a night superimposed on the day because it was winter.

She was walking along enveloped in her sixteen-year-old halo. Marcia was blonde, small, chubby, somewhere between child and adult. She was wearing a wool skirt and a thick blue sweater, with lace-up shoes. Her face was flushed from her walk, but it was always ruddy anyway. She knew her movements made her seem out of place; she could have been just another member of one of the gangs, where girls like her were not infrequent, chatting and laughing, but she didn't know anyone in Flores. She looked like a girl who was going somewhere and had to pass through. It was a miracle no one had handed her any fliers; she was given them every day, but for some strange reason not this time; all the people handing them out had been looking the other way when she passed. It was as if she were a ghost, invisible. But that only increasingly made her the empty center of everyone's gaze and conversations ... if they could be called conversations. If nothing was aimed at her, it was because all directions had vanished. They were a swarm of unknown teenagers ...

"Hey, I'm talking to you ..."

"To me?"

"Wannafuck?"

Two girls had split off from the large group outside the Duncan, and began to follow her. Before too long they caught up with her, because Marcia wasn't far ahead. One of them was talking to her, the other was her sidekick, listening eagerly a few steps behind. When eventually she made out who was speaking, Marcia came to a halt and looked at her:

"Are you crazy?"

"No."

They were two punks, dressed in black. Very young, although maybe slightly older than she was, with pale, childish features. The one doing the talking was very close to her.

"You're gorgeous and I want to fuck you."

"Are you out of your mind?"

She glanced at the other one, who looked the same and was very serious. It didn't seem like a joke. She didn't know them, or at least couldn't recognize them beneath their disguises. There was something serious but insane about the pair of them, about the situation. Marcia couldn't get over her astonishment. She looked away and kept on walking, but the punk grabbed her by the arm.

"You're the one I've been waiting for, you fat cow. Don't make things difficult. I want to lick your cunt, for starters!"

Marcia freed herself at once, and turned her head to answer her a second time.

"You're nuts."

"Come to that dark spot," she said, pointing to Calle Gavilán, which was in fact pitch-black, lined with huge trees. "I want to kiss you."

"Leave me alone."

She set off again, and the two stood where they were, apparently giving up, but the one talking raised her voice, as people always do when somebody walks away, even when they are still close by. Vaguely alarmed, Marcia realized *a posteriori* that this stranger had been speaking loudly right from the start, and the some of the others had heard her and were laughing. Not just the kids, but the flower-seller as well, an elderly man, a grand-dad, whom Marcia brushed past in her flight. He was looking on with great interest, but did not allow it to show on his face, as if he were not entitled to react. He would do so later, when he talked to his female customers; there would be no stopping him with his "degenerates," his "you won't guess what hap-pened," et cetera. "They must have been on drugs," the old la-dies would say. How thoughtless these girls were, Marcia was surprised to find herself thinking. How reckless! How they un-dermined youth! The boys who had heard didn't seem to care in the slightest about that; they were laughing and shouting, thinking it was great.

The two punks were some way away. Without meaning to, Marcia had sped up a little. A bit further on, the music was louder, and some boys standing in the record store doorway were looking at her curiously. They might not have heard, but could have guessed, if not the exact meaning of what was go-ing on, at least how strange it was. Or perhaps she wasn't the first person those two had approached: maybe it was a joke in bad taste that they made all the time. She didn't turn to look, but guessed that the two punks had rejoined one of the small groups and were laughing as they waited for their next victim.

A few more steps, and Marcia had reached the loudest spot. But now the music changed meaning. It was as though it had become real, something that never happened with music. And the reality prevented her from hearing it. She too was thinking at her loudest, so it was also as if her thinking had become real. Where she was now there were still clusters of kids, but as before they no longer paid her any attention (the entire incident had lasted only a few seconds, it was almost as if she had not stopped) but now they were no longer emblems of beauty or happiness, but of *something else.*

Everything had changed. Marcia was shaking from delayed shock. Her heart was in her mouth. She was dumbstruck with astonishment, although since she wasn't in the habit of talking to herself, this wasn't obvious. But the effect was already wearing off, had worn off. The shock was delayed because there had been no time for it while the event was taking place; but afterward, there was no reason for it, it was a fictional shock. Marcia wasn't hysterical, or even nervous or impressionable, or paranoid; she was quite calm and rational.

No, that wasn't where the change was. The atmosphere, the weight of reality had changed. Not because it had become more or less real, but because it seemed that now, anything could happen. Wasn't it like that before? Before, it was as though nothing could happen. It was the system of beauty and happiness of the young people. It was the reason why they gathered there at that time of day, it was their way of making the neighborhood, the city, the night, real. All of a sudden everything was different, as if a cloud of gas had been released. It was incredible how everything could change, thought Marcia, even the smallest details.

There was no need for catastrophes or cataclysms ... On the contrary, an earthquake or a flood would be the surest way of keeping things as they were, of preserving values.

That two girls, two women, should have wanted to pick her up, voicing obscenities out loud, two punks who confirmed their violent self-expulsion from proper behavior ... It was so unexpected, so novel ... Really, anything could happen, and those who could make it happen were the hundreds of young people who came out into the street to waste time at nightfall, after school. They could do anything. They could make night fall in broad daylight. They could set the world spinning, and infinitely slow down Marcia's walk in a straight line (apart from where there was a bend in Rivadavia) from Caballito to Flores.

Marcia was one of those girls of her age who could swear that they are victims. Even though they're not, they could swear to it. Maybe that was why they had picked her out. There are not many like her, even though there are a lot of virgins. A virgin is surrounded by an atmosphere filled with possibilities, looks, time, messages ... If she doesn't appear to be one, then the atmosphere is purer, more transparent, everything flows that much more quickly. If she does look it, as was Marcia's case, the one in a million, that atmosphere can burst into reality. All the faces around her, all the floating, self-absorbed, exhibitionist bodies had become weighted with stories or possibilities for stories, like the myriad of tales she was wandering through ...

She had not taken five steps and she was already completely calm again. In her heart she felt something like a shadow of euphoria: that is the infallible effect of reality. She raised her eyes and all the lights of the avenue were shining just for her against a dense black background. There was still a glow in the sky on the horizon. It didn't matter that they had said it as a joke, which was the only plausible explanation. Just having said it was enough, whatever had been their intention. To have said it was irreversible. It was a click, and everything else was left behind. That meant the two punks had been left behind, definitively, like a sign that had been not only used but well-used: so well in fact that the entire world was its meaning.

But in reality they had not been left behind. Marcia had not gone twenty feet, and was still within the radius of The Cure's music, when they caught up with her.

"Wait a minute, are you in such a hurry?"

"Huh?"

"Are you deaf or just plain dumb?"

Marcia swallowed hard. She had come to a stop. She turned around halfway, and they were face-to-face. Just as before, the one who talked was in front, the other a step further back, to one side. They both looked very serious.

"Did what I said annoy you? Was there something wrong with it?"

"Of course!"

"Don't be such an old maid."

"Get lost, will you? Leave me alone."

"Sorry. If you're angry, I'm sorry." She paused. "What happened? Did I scare you?"

"Me? Why?"

The stranger shrugged and said:

"If you want me to get lost, I will."

It was Marcia's turn to shrug her shoulders. Of course she didn't want to offend anyone. But why was she to blame?

"Did you think it was a joke?"

The question was so accurate she felt in some way duty bound to respond. Otherwise she would have walked on at once. A lot of things had happened during their previous dialogue. What had emerged most clearly was that it wasn't exactly a joke.

"That was a possibility," she said. "But I don't think so now."

"If some guy had said that to you, would you have thought it? That it was a joke?"

"A little bit less."

She said this without thinking, but it was true. The girl pulled a face.

"Don't you believe in love?"

"In love, yes."

"So what did I say?"

"It doesn't matter. Ciao."

She took a step.

"Wait a moment. What's your name?"

"Marcia."

The punk stared at her with that serious, neutral expression of theirs. It was a heavy silence, although she could never have said what made it so heavy. At any rate, it was one of those silences that make you wait. It didn't even occur to her to walk away. She wouldn't have been able to anyway, because the silence only lasted a few seconds.

"What a lovely name. Listen to me, Marcia: what I told you is true. Love at first sight. It's *completely true.* Everything you might think ... is *true.*"

"What's your name?"

"Mao."

" 'Mao?' You're crazy."

"Why?"

"Just because."

"No, tell me why."

"I can't explain."

"Do you believe in love between women?"

"If I'm honest, no I don't."

"But hang on, Marcia, I don't mean platonic love."

"Yes, I realized that."

"And you don't believe in it?"

"But why did this have to happen to me?"

"You know why."

Marcia looked at her, eyes wide with astonishment.

"Because you are you," Mao explained. "Because you're the one I love."

Impossible to hold a rational conversation with her. Was the other one the same? Somehow Mao could follow her thought, or possibly her gaze, and made a brief introduction:

"She's called Lenin. We're lovers."

The other punk nodded.

"But don't get me wrong, Marcia. We're not a couple. We're free. Like you. When I saw you on that corner, I fell in love. The same could have happened to her, and I would understand."

"Okay, that's fine," said Marcia. "It's not my thing. I'm really sorry. Bye. Will you leave me in peace now? People are waiting for me."

"Don't lie! Give me time. Don't you like sex? Don't you do it ... ?"

"How do you expect me to talk about something like that with a stranger in the street? I'm not interested in sex without love."

"You misunderstood me, Marcia. Don't talk about sex, because that has nothing to do with it. What I want is to go to bed with you, kiss you on the mouth, suck those fat tits of yours, hug you like a doll ... "

Marcia turned pale. She decided to turn round and head off without another word, but was afraid they might make a scene.

"I'm not a lesbian."

"Nor am I."

A pause.

"Look: I want to go ..."

Her voice sounded oddly strangulated. Mao must have thought she was about to burst into tears, because her attitude and tone of voice changed abruptly.

"Don't be such a drama queen. We're not going to eat you. I'd never do anything to hurt you. Because I love you. That's what I'm trying to get you to understand. I love you."

"Why do you say that?" asked Marcia in a whisper.

"Because it's true."

"Anybody else would have told you to get lost."

"But not you."

"Because I'm stupid. Excuse me, I want to go."

"Do you have a boyfriend?"

What a ridiculous question, at this point in the proceedings! "No."

"You see? Anybody else would have said yes, he's a weight lifter and he's waiting for me on the next corner. But you told me the truth."

"What does that prove? That I'm even stupider than I thought, and I don't know how to get rid of the pair of you."

"Listen, Marcia, does it upset you that Lenin is here? Do you want her to leave so the two of us can talk on our own?"

"No! No, I'm the one who wants to leave." She thought for a moment: "Aren't you ashamed of treating your friend like that, your 'lover' as you call her?"

"I'd do the same for her, and a lot more. An awful lot more. Don't get it wrong, Marcia, we're not a couple of sluts."

"Did you make a bet?" Marcia looked in the direction they had come from. The possibility had just occurred to her. But nobody was watching them.

"Don't talk crap. I'm not such an asshole."

Marcia gave her that. She didn't know why, but she conceded it.

"Okay ..." she said with a smile. The conversation had gone on long enough. "Pleasure meeting you ..."

"Allow me just one more question, Marcia. I've already asked lots, so one more won't hurt. Do you know what love is?"

"I think so."

"Have you ever been in love?"

"No."

"Can I ask you a more intimate question?"

"No, but thanks for asking. In the end, you're not that much of a brute, are you? It's like you weren't a real punk."

"Would you like it if all three of us went to bed together?" asked Lenin. This was the first thing she had said. Her voice was soft and pleasant.

"You too?" said Marcia despairingly.

The two punks talked between themselves.

"Do you like her?" asked Mao.

"I didn't at first, but I do a bit more now."

"She's so different from us."

"I do like her now, I could fall in love with her."

Marcia wasn't upset by this exchange; on the contrary, for the first time it made her feel almost at ease. Mao turned resolutely toward her, as though something important had taken place.

"Lenin is good, she's passionate, she's made me come a lot. I always listen to her because she's intelligent, much more than I am. Did you hear what she said? She confirmed me in my opinion. It's settled. It was before anyway, but I wasn't completely certain. What can I do to convince you?"

This was a question that called for a reply, a concrete reply. Marcia thought about it.

"Let me go."

"No. I want the opposite. I want you to say yes, to throw yourself into my arms. But this isn't getting us anywhere. Would you like the three of us just to talk, about anything, not love, like friends? What do girls like you talk about? Do you want us to go window shopping? Don't say someone is waiting for you, because it's not true. I'm not going to try to pick you up. You can't deny us a little bit of your time."

"What for?"

"Just because; to add something to life, to get to know people …"

"No, I mean what would *you* do it for?"

"I won't lie: I'm doing it to gain time, because I love you and I want to fuck you. But that can wait."

Marcia said nothing.

"What's your problem?" asked Mao.

All of a sudden Marcia felt free, almost happy.

"Well …" she said hesitantly. "I've always wanted to get to know a punk, but I've never had the opportunity."

"Good. At last you're being reasonable."

"But don't get your hopes up."

"I'll worry about that."

"One more thing: I want you to promise me that if at the end I say good-bye and leave, which is what I'm going to do, you two won't follow me and make a scene. More than that: I want you to promise that if right now I say good-bye and leave, you won't move an inch."

"Listen Marcia, it would be very easy to promise you that or anything else. But I won't. I won't make a scene, or do anything bad to you, *anything*, I promise, but I'm not going to let you go. Would it be love if I promised you that? It's for your own good. Besides, you yourself say you wanted to get to know punks. Are you going to get another opportunity?" When she saw Marcia's impatient reaction, she raised her hand to calm her, and added: "Let's go back to what we agreed, and talk about something else."

"Let's go to Pumper," said Lenin.

She set off across the street right there, in the middle of the block, striding between the cars and dragging the other two after her. Marcia glanced at Mao out of the corner of her eye: she seemed distracted, as if she was thinking of something else. She admired her for never once smiling; she herself always smiled, because she was nervous, and she hated the habit.

Inside the Pumper Nic it was a blaze of white neon light, and the heat was on full blast. The three of them entered together, or rather in a straggling line, with Mao bringing up the rear. Were they surrounding her in case she tried to escape? No, that couldn't be it. They went in like three friends: two of one kind, the third of another. Marcia felt calm and almost happy. Putting an end to the scene outside was a relief. It was as if they were entering another more normal and predictable stage. They attracted stares from the few customers there; people were always curious about punks. Since the other two took the lead, Marcia was able to study them as the others were doing. Dressed in black from head to foot, with thin black jeans; Mao had on a man's black jacket over a t-shirt made of some strange heavy cloth, and black sneakers. Lenin was wearing a worn leather jacket and boots without laces, all in black as well. They both had lots of ugly metal necklaces and pins around their necks, and chains around their waists and wrists. Their hair was half shaven and half long strands dyed red, brick-red, and purple. Confrontational, taking on the world, dangerous (or so they would like to think). What impression would they make on this ultranormal public of youngsters, adults and children busy eating their hamburgers and drinking soft drinks? Would they feel invaded, threatened? Marcia could not avoid the childish satisfaction of thinking they were jealous of her for being with them, for having access to their strange way of being and thinking. Perhaps they would think they were childhood friends who had taken different paths in life, and had gotten together to exchange experiences. Or maybe they thought (after all, it was more logical) that she was a punk too, except that her hair and clothes were conventional. She quickened her pace to catch up with the others: she didn't want anyone making a mistake and thinking it was only a coincidence she had come in with them. An assistant was polishing the floor; they stepped on the cord of his machine as if it wasn't there. Marcia didn't step on it; it seemed so natural for her to avoid it that her companions' surprise seemed almost supernatural. Unless they were putting it on, but that didn't seem likely.

There was a long corridor with tables that led from the first room to another one at the back, where a children's birthday party was being held. Her guides in black did not go very far down it, but sat at a big table before the halfway point. Fortunately the tables on either side were empty. There wasn't much risk of them being heard anyway because of the music and the din from the children's party. What was more disturbing was their behavior: Mao leaned against the wall and put her feet up on the chair. She was on her own on one side, because Marcia sat down opposite her, next to Lenin; it seemed to be the rule that she had to turn to talk to her, and she didn't question it. The first thing Marcia said as they were sitting down was an instinctive reaction:

"You have to order up at the counter."

"What the fuck do I care."

Marcia realized she had gone too far in persuading herself that things were more normal now. Going into the Pumper Nic in a group, like the local schoolgirls did, had led her to believe they were going to behave like everyone else, even if only to use this as a backdrop for an explanation. But it wasn't going to be like that. They had no intention of ordering anything, and that was only to be expected. Punks didn't do fast food. She recalled having seen them drinking straight from big bottles of beer in doorways.

"We'll get thrown out if we don't have something," she said.

"I'd like to see them dare say a single word to me," said Mao, peering round with a look of profound scorn.

"We said there'd be no scenes."

The two punks looked at her with neutral, serious expressions. That expression, which expressed nothing, was one of pure violence. They were violence. There was no escaping the fact. She wasn't going to emerge from her audience with the punks scot-free, as she had absentmindedly thought. It was not the same as with any other strange specimen in society, which could be provided with a favorable setting in which to ask questions. Because they themselves were the setting. She resigned herself to it: she had never set foot in this Pumper before, and had no problem with never coming back if they were thrown out.

But the so-called Mao had an idea and didn't keep it to herself:

"Do you want something, Marcia? A coke, a beer?"

This had its funny side. She was asking her if she "wanted something," and that was one of the classic pick-up lines.

"Do you want to tell us what the fuck you're laughing at, *Marcia*?"

"I remembered a joke I heard from Porcel on TV the other night. In the sketch where he's a newspaper seller. An old Spanish guy comes up and tells him he was once at the San Fermín fiesta in Pamplona. They let the bulls loose, and he started running. He was running, with the bull right behind him ... him in front, the bull behind ... When they came to a corner, the King was going by. So he, like the good subject he was, bowed low before him ... and the bull ... so Porcel asks him: Just like that? Without inviting him for a drink first?"

She burst out laughing, but the others didn't join in. They didn't even smile.

"Who is Porcel?" asked Lenin.

"You don't know Fatty Porcel?"

"He's a guy on TV," Mao explained to Lenin.

"And is he fat? His name must mean 'porker.'"

"Just out of curiosity," said Marcia, "did you get the joke?"

"Yes," said Mao. "The bull stuck a horn up his arse. If that's a joke ..."

"It was funny because of the way he said it, the improvisation. I don't know how to tell jokes."

Mao sighed and straightened up opposite her, as if she were resigned to saying something completely banal:

"You told it very well. But it's difficult for something like that to be funny, Marcia. You must tell yourself those jokes very well, you're always laughing."

"I laugh because I'm nervous, not because something's funny. Not just now: always. I admire people who can stay serious no matter what dreadful things happen to them."

"That's paradoxical. You're very intelligent, Marcia. It's good to talk to an intelligent person for a change."

"You don't have intelligent friends?"

"I don't have friends."

"Nor do I," said Lenin.

Marcia preferred to change tack:

"Do you really not watch TV?"

Neither of them deigned to reply. Mao had slumped back in her chair. Where was the supervisor who would come to tell her to take her feet off the chair, or to throw them out if they weren't going to have anything? Marcia was sitting with her back to the counter, and so couldn't see the preparations that must be underway to expel them.

"Whatever," said Mao, "we couldn't buy you anything because we have no dough."

"I do. But I don't know if it's enough to buy beer or hamburgers. It's expensive here …"

She paused when she realized her words had fallen flat. A silence followed.

"Thanks, *Marcia,* don't worry about it."

"Why do you repeat my name all the time?"

"Because I like it. I like it more than I can explain. Of all the stupid names they give women, it's the only one I like, and I've only just discovered it."

"You don't like any names?" Marcia asked her, trying to head off the fresh declaration of love she could sense coming.

"None. They're all ridiculous."

"What are you called? Really, I mean."

"Nothing. Mao. Lenin."

"And you think ordinary names are ridiculous! I'd say you're called ... Amalia ... and Elena. How strange, they're my favorites. And I've just discovered that too."

"That's not what we're called," said Lenin-Elena, as if Marcia had really tried to guess.

But Mao-Amalia suddenly sprang back to life and silenced her from the far side of the table.

"Would you like us to be called Amalia and Elena? Because if that's the case, consider it done. It's not in the least important to us."

"Is that so? Do you change names every day, just like that? To the name that the person you're with prefers?"

"No. In that case we would choose the name that 'person' as you call them hates most."

It was Lenin who had spoken, and she did so with a touch of irony that was refreshing against the background of mortal seriousness they gave everything. And when Mao spoke again, it was just as seriously:

"Which doesn't mean we can't change names as often as we damn well like. But I'm telling you, Marcia, that from tomorrow on the two of us, Lenin and I, we're going to call ourselves 'Marcia'. What do you think?"

"Why from tomorrow on?" asked Marcia.

"Because tomorrow will be an important day in our lives," she replied cryptically.

They fell silent again for a moment. Mao was staring at her.

Marcia looked away, but not before she noticed something very odd, which she could not define there and then. The silence dragged on, as if the three of them had thought the same thing, and none of them knew what it was. Eventually Mao, like someone carrying out a painful obligation, but in a friendly way, addressed Marcia:

"What did you want to know about us?"

Marcia had no time even to begin to think what questions she wanted to ask, because at that moment the Pumper supervisor appeared at their table. She had dyed blonde hair, and was wearing a white blouse and gray miniskirt.

"If you're not going to have anything you can't stay."

Marcia was about to tell her that in fact she was going to order an ice cream (the idea occurred to her at that very instant) but her jaw dropped before she could emit a sound because Mao got in before her:

"Go fuck yourself."

The supervisor looked stunned, although on second thought what else could she have expected? She seemed lively: she was very attractive, about twenty-five years old. The kind of woman who wouldn't be pushed around, Marcia decided.

"What?"

"Fuck off and leave us in peace. We need to talk."

"Start by taking your foot off the chair."

Mao responded by removing both feet and scraping them noisily.

"That all right? Now leave us in peace. Move."

The supervisor turned on her heel and walked away. Marcia was astounded. She couldn't help admiring the punks. In theory, she was not unaware that other people could be treated that way; but in practice she had never tried it, and it wasn't something she planned to do. She told herself that when it came to it, reality was more theoretical than thought.

When she came out of this momentary reflection, it was as if the nature of Pumper had changed. It wasn't the first time she felt this since the two girls had stopped her on the sidewalk, less than a quarter of an hour earlier: the world had been transformed time and again. It seemed like a permanent feature of the effect they had on it. It would be logical to presume that this effect would wear off the longer it went on; no one is an everlasting box of surprises, and despite the strangeness of the two punks, she could make out a shallow depth to them: the vulgarity of two lost girls playing a role. Once the play was over there would be nothing left, no secret, they would be as boring as a chemistry class ... And yet at the same time she could imagine the opposite, even though as yet she didn't know why: maybe the world, once it has been transformed, can no longer stop changing.

"Wait for me a minute," she said, getting up. "I'm going to ask for an ice cream. That way they won't bother us anymore."

"If that's the reason, don't worry," said Mao. "No one's going to bother you. We'll make sure of that."

"But I *want* an ice cream," said Marcia, only half lying. "Don't you want one?"

"No."

She went to the front counter. She had to wait a while for the assistant to serve several coffees and teas with slices of cake. She was by the door, and nothing could have been easier than to leave, run to the corner, or catch a bus ... Back at the table, neither of them were looking in her direction. But she didn't want to escape. Or rather, she did want to, but not until she had found out more about them. So she waited her turn patiently, ordered an ice cream with a chocolate topping, and came back with it on a tray. All at once she really felt like having one. An ice cream in winter accentuated things; and a half truth that became the complete truth accentuated them still further. The supervisor who had threatened them passed by, in such a busy rush she didn't even look at Marcia. It was as though everybody was thinking about something else, and doubtless they were. Wasn't it true that after a certain length of time everybody did think about something else? Added to the ice cream, the idea comforted her. She sat back down with her friends and tasted it.

"Delicious," she said.

The other two looked at her absentmindedly, as though from a long way off. Were they thinking of something else too? Had they forgotten their intentions? Marcia picked at the chocolate topping rather anxiously, but didn't have to wait long for things to get back on track.

"What did you want to ask us, Marcia?" Mao reminded her.

"To be honest, nothing in particular. Besides, I don't think you can give me answers. In general, questions and answers aren't the best way to find out about things."

"What do you mean?"

"In abstract terms, I'd like to know what punks think, why they become punks; all that. But at the same time I ask myself: why do I want to know that, what does it matter to me?"

It was all very logical, very rational, and she could have carried on a long time in that vein, until she had turned the whole situation into a "Marcian" one. Good try! Mao made sure she burst that balloon right away.

"How fuckin' stupid you are, Marcia."

"Why?" And then, correcting herself at once (correcting herself because there was no correcting Mao). "Yes, I am stupid. You're right. I should become a punk if I want to know what it means, and to know why I want to know."

"No." Mao interrupted her with a sarcastic, humorless little laugh. "You're completely wrong. You're far more stupid than even you imagine. We're not 'punks.'"

"What are you then?"

"You would never get it."

"Besides," Lenin interrupted her, in her less abrupt manner, "don't you think it's absurd to think *you* could become a punk. Have you looked at yourself in the mirror?"

"Are you saying that because I'm ... overweight?" asked Marcia, who was hurt and whose eyes showed it despite herself.

Lenin seemed almost about to smile:

"Just the opposite ..."

"Just the opposite," Mao repeated fervently. "How can you not see it?"

She paused for an instant, and Marcia's astonishment floated in the air.

"You were right," Lenin said finally to her friend, "she's incredibly stupid."

Marcia ate a spoonful of ice cream. She felt at ease enough to try another topic.

"What do you mean you're not punks?" The only response was a click of the tongue from Mao. "For example, don't you like The Cure?"

Like two sphinxes. Lenin deigned to ask:

"What's that?"

"The English group, the musicians. I like them. Robert Smith is a genius."

"Never heard them."

"He's that cretin who wears lipstick and makeup. I saw him on the cover of a magazine."

"What an asshole."

"But it's theater," stammered Marcia, "it's ... provocation, that's all. I don't think he wears makeup because he likes it. The look is part of the philosophy he represents ..."

"He's still an asshole."

"Do you prefer heavy metal?"

"We don't prefer anything, Marcia."

"You don't like music?"

"Music is idiotic."

"Freddie Mercury is idiotic?"

"Of course."

"What nihilists you are. I can't believe you really think that."

Mao's eyes narrowed and she said nothing. Marcia returned to the charge:

"What do you like then?"

Mao's eyes narrowed still further (they were almost completely shut by now) and still said nothing. Lenin sighed and said:

"The answer you're expecting is 'nothing'. But we're not going to say 'nothing'. You're going to have to go on asking questions, although you may think they won't get you anywhere."

"I give up."

"Congratulations," said Mao. She relaxed and opened her eyes to look around her. "What a dump. Do you know something, Marcia? In places like this where there are waitresses who have to be single to get the job, there's always at least one who's pregnant. So there's always at least one tragedy in the offing."

"They're feminists," thought Marcia while Mao was saying this. It was a small, automatic conclusion that rather disappointed her. She looked up from her ice cream and saw that one of the uniformed girls sweeping up was staring at them. She was studying them with great curiosity, and not trying to hide it. She was almost as young as they were, short, fair-haired and plump, with the ruddy complexion of a European peasant girl. Marcia felt strangely uneasy under her scrutiny. Because she looked extraordinarily like her: they were exactly the same type. She felt an irrational urge to hide her from her two friends. The waitress diminished her own value; Mao and Lenin might see she wasn't the only one cut from that cloth. But the punks' minds were elsewhere. They had seen her and not noticed the likeness (there wasn't in fact a likeness, it was more the fact of belonging to the same type). Mao said to her:

"Now you'll see," and called the girl over. She came at once. "I said I'd bring …" she told her, "a sweater and some booties to a girl who works here and is pregnant, but I can't remember her name. Which one is it?"

"Pregnant?"

"Yes. Are you deaf, you fat cow?"

"It's Matilde who's pregnant."

"So?"

"A tall, dark girl."

"That's the one," Mao lied.

"She's on the morning shift. She's already left. We have three shifts, in rotation …"

"What the fuck is that to me? Thanks. Ciao."

"Do you want to leave the things for her?"

"And have them stolen? No. On your way. Give me room to breathe."

The waitress would gladly have continued the conversation. She didn't seem in the least bit offended by Mao's rudeness.

"How did you meet her?"

"What fuckin' business is that of yours? Get lost; we have to talk."

"Okay. Don't get mad. It was you who asked me a question."

"What's your name?" Lenin asked.

"Liliana."

"How much do you make?"

"The minimum wage."

"How stupid you all are," said Mao. "I don't understand why you work."

"I work to help out my family. And I study."

"What?"

"Medicine."

"Don't make me laugh. Carry on sweeping, doctor," said Mao.

"I have to finish college."

"Of course. And high school as well."

"No, I finished high school. I'm in the third year of college. When I finish here I go to evening classes. I make sacrifices to get ahead. The problem with this country is that no one wants to work."

Mao straightened in her seat and glared directly at Liliana.

"You've no idea how sick you make me feel. Get lost, before I hit you."

"Why would you do that? Besides, I'd fight back. I've got a strong character."

She said all this with the humble voice of someone sleep-walking. She seemed half idiotic, half slow-witted. There was one way she was different from Marcia: she didn't smile. She went off still sweeping the floor, but as if to say: I'll be right back.

"What a dummy," said Lenin.

"Why?" said Marcia. "There must be a lot like her. Working and studying … We should have asked her if she had a boyfriend."

"Didn't you see she's deformed? Who's going to want to fuck a monster like that!"

Marcia's surprise only grew. From surprise she went to surprise within surprise. Not only had Liliana not seemed deformed to her (on the contrary, she had been struck by her self-assured normality, often found in dimwitted people), but she had seen her as her own double. Marcia was typically young in that she could only see love as a question of general types; you fell in love with a set of characteristics that you found in a certain individual, but could also exist in another somebody else. You only had to find the one possessing them. For the young, that is love; that is why they are so restless, so sociable, always searching; because love can be anywhere, everywhere; for them, the whole world is love.

But if the punks had not fallen in love with the type she represented … what was it then? Where was the key? Mao had told her she had been waiting for her, that she had only to see her to know she loved her. That meant she knew what she was like, what she ought to be. But now that didn't seem to be the case.

Still confused by all this, she came to Liliana's defence:

"You're wrong," she told Mao. "She's not deformed, or ugly, and I bet she does have a boyfriend. No, don't call her over," she said, seeing Mao stirring. "It doesn't matter what she might say. Tell me the truth: isn't she pretty in her own way? She's childish, and a bit slow, but there are dozens of boys who like that type. She could make you feel you want to protect her, for example …"

"She makes me feel I want to crush her like an insect."

"Can't you see? There are people who get married for less than that." She paused, then took a risk: "In fact, that's my only hope of not turning into an old maid. Didn't you notice that she's the same kind as me?"

The look Mao gave her froze her blood. Marcia had the ghastly feeling that Mao had been reading her mind all this time. More than that: she had deliberately been leading her on, that all this had been a sadistic maneuver. She quickly changed subjects.

"Why were you so aggressive? Why did you treat her so badly, when she seemed so sweet?"

"No one is sweet deep down," said Lenin (her companion seemed to reserve herself for more important declarations).

"That's a preconception. Nobody is going to be sweet toward *you* if you think and act the way you do. You have to be more optimistic."

"Don't talk crap," said Mao, who had apparently decided that the time for important declarations had arrived. "You're play-acting. Imitating that poor dummy. 'I make sacrifices …' her sort need to be destroyed."

"Why?"

"Because she suffers. So that she won't suffer anymore."

"But she doesn't suffer. She wants to be a doctor, to be happy. She's … innocent. She seemed very nice and sweet to me. I'd help her if I could, rather than insult her like you did. She thinks everyone is good deep down, and probably still thinks so, despite the way you two treated her."

"She can think what she likes. But I'm sure she'd plunge a knife in my back at the first opportunity."

"No, I don't think so."

"If she dared to, she would. The only help I'd be happy to give her is to teach her how to stab people in the back. That would be more useful to her than becoming a doctor."

"I think I understand something now," said Marcia. "What you want is for evil to rule in this world. You want to destroy innocence."

"Don't talk nonsense."

"We don't want anything," said Lenin.

"Nothing?"

"Nothing like that. It's useless."

Useless? That gave Marcia a hint:

"Does that mean there are other things, other actions, that are useful? What are they?"

"You really get my goat with all your blah-blah," said Mao. "That's a good example of uselessness."

"So what is useful then? What's the point of living? Tell me, please."

"You're playing at being Liliana. I won't talk to you until you are yourself again."

This was true, up to a point. Except that Marcia didn't think she could get anywhere (and not only on this occasion, but always) if she didn't swap roles, adopt other characters. Otherwise she finished up in dead ends, fell into the abyss, was paralyzed with fear. At that moment it occurred to her that perhaps that fear was something she had to confront, to accept. That could be the lesson of this punk nihilism. But she didn't believe it; on the one hand, her two companions would deny that they had any lesson to give her; on the other, they themselves, in the disguises they had adopted, were a rebuttal of that morality, despite the fact that it wasn't so ridiculous, given the mutable atmosphere that they operated in.

"All right," she said. "But before I give up being Liliana, there's something I want to say: I identify with her through innocence. I couldn't care less what nonsense she might talk, nor the pity she might inspire: she is innocent, and I'd like to be just as innocent as her. I probably am. You say nobody would fuck her. You're completely wrong, but that doesn't matter. Let's say she is a virgin ... like me." She paused: if this wasn't the abyss, it was something very like it. Neither of the others said anything. "When you two intercepted me, I was walking around in a world where seduction was very discreet, very invisible. Everything that was being said and was going on in the street were signs of seduction, because the world seduces a virgin, but nothing was aimed specifically at me. Then you two appeared, with your abrupt: wannafuck? It was as if innocence became personified, not exactly in you or in me, but in the situation, in the words (I can't explain it). Before then, the world was talking, but saying nothing. Afterward, when you said that, innocence removed her mask. Now look at Liliana. She represents the same thing, and sometimes I think there's no such thing as coincidence. She talks of her life as if it were natural to do so. It's another way of speaking, even more violent than yours, if you like. At first I thought she put me in the shade, but in fact it's you two she diminishes. Although in the end it's the same innocence, and that innocence is the only thing I can understand."

"That means you don't understand a thing," Mao interrupted her with a gesture of distant disdain characteristic of her. "There's nothing more to say."

"I don't understand why you refuse to discuss these things!"

"You will, I promise you. Have you finished?"

"Yes."

"I'm glad. Let's talk about something else."

They fell silent for a moment. The Pumper had started to fill up, and this reassured Marcia, because they were more easily hidden in the crowd. But if all the tables became occupied, which seemed likely to happen soon, someone would come and throw the three of them out. She had finished the ice cream. As if it were a charm to prevent them from being interrupted, Marcia quickly raised another question she thought might lead somewhere:

"Earlier today, opposite here, were you with someone?"

"No. I already told you, we were on our own."

"There were so many people …"

"We'd mixed with those stupid kids to see if we could pick somebody up, but we didn't know anyone and didn't have time to choose because right then you appeared ..."

This information offered a few interesting elements, but seemed deliberately to ensure that they were of the kind Marcia preferred not to pursue. So she continued along the same line she had already taken.

"Do you belong to some group or other?"

"What does that mean?"

"I mean some group of punks."

"No," said Mao, venomously emphasizing every word she said: 'We're not part of any carnival band."

"I didn't mean it badly. People always like to associate with others who share their ideas, their tastes, their way of being."

"Like you and Liliana, for example? Do you belong to a group of innocents?"

"Don't try to twist what I'm saying. And don't pretend not to understand. Here and everywhere else in the world punks get together and support each other in their rejection of society."

"Bravo for your erudition. The answer is no."

"But you do know other punks?"

She was proud of her own question. She should have asked it right at the start. It was a perfect lure. It was as though someone asked them if they knew other human beings. If they denied it, which is obviously what they wanted to do, that would show their bad faith. She had no idea what good that would do her, but at least she would have an answer.

Mao's eyes narrowed once more. She was too intelligent not to spot how great the danger was. But she wouldn't let herself be forced into anything. Ever.

"Why is that important?" she said. "Why are you always trying to get us to talk about what we're not interested in?"

"We made a pact. We made an agreement."

"All right. What was your question?"

Marcia said implacably:

"If you know other punks."

Mao, to Lenin:

"Do you know any?"

"There's Sergio Vicio."

"Oh yes, of course, Sergio ..." She turned to Marcia. "He's an acquaintance of ours. We haven't seen him for ages, but he's an excellent example. Shame we don't have a photo of him. He was the bass guitarist in a band; he was always high, and was a great kid. He still must be, though he's a little bit crazy, out of it. When he talks, which isn't very often, you can't understand a word. Something extraordinary happened to him once. A very rich woman went to a party, and among other things she was wearing a pair of earrings that had four emeralds as big as saucers on each of them. All of a sudden she realized that one was missing; and even though they turned over all the sofas and carpets, they couldn't find it. Since it cost millions, and rich women are very concerned about their possessions, which always cost millions, there was a huge scandal, which even got into the papers. All the guests agreed to allow themselves to be

searched on the way out, apart from the Paraguayan ambassador, who refused and wasn't frisked. Of course, that made him
the prime suspect. The foreign ministry got involved, and the
ambassador was recalled to his country and lost his post. A year
later, the same lady went to a party at the Palladium. Imagine
her surprise when on the dance floor she spotted Sergio Vicio,
with the four emeralds dangling from one ear. Her bodyguards
went after him at once and brought him back by the scruff of
his neck. She was with a colonel, the Interior Minister, Pirker,
and Mitterrand's wife. They brought another chair and made
Sergio Vicio sit down. As they had been talking in French at the
table, the lady in question asked him if he spoke the language.
Sergio said he did. 'Some time ago,' she told him, 'I lost an earring that was identical to yours. I wonder if this is the same
one?' Sergio looked at her, but couldn't see (or hear) her. He
had been dancing three or four hours nonstop, something he
often does because he loves to dance, and when the movement
ended all of a sudden he had a problem with his blood pressure.
This was the first time it had happened to him, because he always instinctively stopped dancing gradually, and then went
out to walk until dawn. The effect of being hauled off the dance
floor left him blind: everything was covered with little red dots
and he couldn't see a thing. It's called orthostatic hypotension,
but he didn't know that. Other symptoms accompanying the
vision loss are nausea, which he didn't get because he hadn't
had a bite to eat in two or three days, and vertigo, which he
was used to because of all the dope he smoked, and which far

from upsetting or alarming him kept him amused during all
the rest of the scene, which he spent rocking himself in cosmic
space. The lady, a light-fingered expert, made the earring disappear from his ear as if it was a magic trick. Now at the party
being held there that night, which was in honor of an ORTF
orchestra visiting Argentina, the Palladium was inaugurating
a system of quartz strobe lights, the cutting edge of technology. And they switched them on at that very moment. At the
table they were so taken up with Sergio Vicio they didn't hear
the announcement. When the lady had taken the earring from
his ear, she held it up by the little hook for all of them to see
and began to say: 'These emeralds ...' She didn't manage to get
any further, because as the new lights hit the stones they made
them completely transparent like the purest crystal. There was
no trace of green in them. Her jaw dropped. 'Emeralds?' said
Mitterrand's wife, 'but they're diamonds. And of the first wa-
ter! I've never seen anything like them.' 'What do you mean,
diamonds?' said Pirker. 'Where would this bum get something
like that? They're bits of glass from some granny's chandelier,
tied together with wire.' Struck dumb, their owner was gasping
like an axolotl. And at that moment, the first bars of *Pierrot Lu-
naire* could be heard. No less a personage than Pierre Boulez
was on stage, with the fantastic Helga Pilarczyk as soprano. The
guests at the table transferred their attention to the music. No
emerald turned into a diamond could compare with the moon-
lit notes of this masterpiece. The most basic elegance dictated
the supremacy of music over gems. Moving like a robot, the

lady copied her previous gesture in reverse, and fixed the earring back on Sergio Vicio's earlobe, then watched in anguished silence as the bodyguards, misinterpreting what was going on, lifted him up and deposited him back on the dance floor. He started dancing again, regardless of the music, until he got his sight back and left to go for a walk, still on automatic pilot. And she never saw her emeralds again."

Silence.

Marcia couldn't believe it. This was the first time in her life that she had heard a well-told story, and it had seemed to her sublime, an experience that made up for all the fears this meeting had caused.

"It's . . . marvelous," she stammered. "I know I ought to thank you, but I can't find the words. You've surprised me far more than I could say . . . While you were talking I felt transported. It was as if I could see everything . . ."

Mao waved her hand dismissively. This was such a new experience for Marcia that she couldn't help thinking of the rules of etiquette there must be in such cases. She had to discover them all on her own, as they went along. To start with, she grasped that it was not okay to go on praising the form; such praise had to be transmitted implicitly in her comments on the content. But she was so dazzled that content and form became intertwined; whatever she might say about the former would inevitably be transferred to the latter. The most practical thing—and what came most naturally to her, were questions, doubts. What happened next to Sergio Vicio? And the earring?

How had he got in to that party at the Palladium? Had the two of them ever been there? Marcia of course had never set foot in the famous nightspot. Probably the punks were allowed in free, even on the most important occasions, to add some local color, as part of the décor. To her, the Palladium had all the hallmarks of something in a dream, and it was no surprise to her that all those famous, important people were there … It was almost another world, but one linked to this one through the fantastic aspect of the tale … Could it be that her friends had been in the Palladium *that night*? How had they heard about what had happened? That was what was important, and to a certain extent that was what the story of the earring was about …

She began asking them questions, which they seemed to find inopportune. Who were the musicians they had mentioned? The only one that sounded well-known to her was the one called Pierrot. She thought she remembered he had played with Tom Verlaine in Television. Mao's art as a narrator had transported her from the plebeian neon lighting of the Pumper to the shadows of this dream, shot through with a lunar glow. She even thought she had heard music she had never heard before, something that almost inconceivably was even better than The Cure and the Rolling Stones …

None of her questions were answered, because a second supervisor had appeared at their table. This one was formidable, threatening, and demanded to be taken into account. She was exactly the sort of person who had to be taken into account. Especially as she was the spitting image of the first supervisor, with each of her features intensified: she was taller, her hair even more dyed; the miniskirt even shorter. She was prettier, sterner, more determined. Whereas the other one seemed like someone who might allow herself to be pushed around (that must be a requisite for the job) this one was the model of a strong character, of energetic initiative.

"Get out."

Her voice left no room for doubt. Marcia would have happily gotten up and left. She glanced at Mao, who slowly raised her eyes toward the intruder like a cobra uncoiling. Here was a worthy opponent. The stage of Lilianas was past. The establishment had kept its heavy artillery for the end.

"What's wrong with you?"

"You have to leave."

"What?" It really was as if Mao were coming out of a dream. "What . . . ? And who are you?"

"The super . . ."

All at once Lenin had an open switchblade in her hand. The blade was eight inches long and sharp as a razor. Marcia blanched. Lenin was sitting on her side, next to the wall. If there was an attack, Marcia was blocking her exit. But it didn't seem as if things would get that far. Mao glanced at her friend and said:

"Put that away, there's no need for it."

"Do you want me to call the police?" said the supervisor, starting to move away.

Mao took her time replying:

"You've got such a fucking ugly bitch's face."

"Do *you* want me to call the police?"

"Yes, please. Go on, call them."

All this, noted Marcia, was said in a paroxysm of violence that revealed a new dimension to the punks ... and also, yet again, to the world. They faced each other like two powerful beasts, both of them sure of their own strength, and even of the balance of power between them, at an excessive level. In confrontations of this sort, victory went to whoever possessed a secret weapon, and it was obvious that in this case it was Mao who had it.

"You were threatening one of the girls ..." said the supervisor.

"Which girl? Liliana? But she's a friend of ours."

Slightly disconcerted, the supervisor looked over at Marcia, who nodded. That was a point in her favor, but it was a shame that Mao immediately threw it away:

"We're waiting for her to finish her shift to go and have a fuck. Do you have a problem with that?"

"Are you making fun of me, you piece of scum?"

"No, shithead. Liliana is a lezzie, and delighted to go to bed with us. Do you want to stop her?"

"I'm going to ask her right now."

"You think she'd tell you the truth? If you do, you've not just a bitch, you're a cretin."

"Liliana gets off at ten, and you're not going to spend hours here."

"We're going to stay as long as we fuckin' well like. Ciao. Go call the cops."

They stared each other out for a moment. The supervisor

moved away, with a look on her face that said: I'll be right back. They all left with the same threat, but never did come back.

When the tense moment had passed and she had recovered the power of speech, Marcia felt completely shocked.

"How could you be such a traitor! You put it all onto poor Liliana! That could cost her the job."

"Why?"

"D'you think they will want a lesbian employee who makes dates with lovers who pull out switchblades?"

"It's all relative, Marcia. Maybe now they'll respect her more. And if they throw her out, she'll find a better job: that's life. That means we've probably done her a favor without meaning to. She didn't seem to me particularly happy with what she's doing. The fact that she spoke to us shows that she is open to other possibilities."

"Possibly," said Marcia, not convinced. "But anyway, I'm not happy about lying. That's always an insult. To me, truth is sacred."

"Not to me."

"Or me," said Lenin.

"So much the worse for you. It devalues everything you've said . . ."

For the first time since they had come in, Mao showed genuine interest, as if Marcia had finally hit on a topic that was worth considering.

"Fine," she said. "So what?"

"What d'you mean, 'so what'?"

"I mean, why is that important?"

"It's important because it is. It's what makes the difference between talking for its own sake and wanting to say something."

Mao shook her head.

"Do you think anything we've said since we sat here is important?"

This was not a completely rhetorical question: she was expecting a reply.

"Yes," said Marcia. "It was important for me."

"Well then, you're mistaken."

"If that's what you think, why bother to speak at all?"

"If for nothing else, to make you understand that, Marcia: that none of it is important. That's it's all nothing, or the same as nothing."

"And you told me you weren't nihilists!"

"We're not. *You* are the nihilist. Could you really spend your life talking crap, worried about the kind of things that happen here, in this hamburger microcosm? All this is accidental, nothing more than the springboard to launch us back to what is important. Which brings us back to our starting point. Are you satisfied now? Have you found out all you wanted to know about us? Can we get back to talking about the other?"

"I don't get you, Mao ..." there was a pleading note to her voice that was completely involuntary. But as she said the punk's name, Marcia once more felt the indefinable something was now closer to her awareness, but still outside it. The restaurant had become unreal, perhaps due to the constant coming and going of adolescents along the corridor, or the dazzling white lighting, or more probably because they had been sitting without moving for a while, which was something Marcia always detested. There was a mirror on the wall, which she looked at for the first time: she was pale, glassy-eyed. The faces of the other two looked veiled. "I don't feel well. I think that ice cream disagreed with me. What time can it be?" Her question fell into an indifferent silence. "Isn't the time important to you either? I guess not. Of course not. Why should it be? What gives you the right to decide what's important for me and what isn't? You don't know me, and I don't know you. Who are you? What do you want?"

"I've already told you that."

What did they want? Who were they? Who was she? Everything was blurred in a corrosive mist. Marcia felt paralyzed. If she moved, she would evaporate like a smoke ring. Okay, so nothing was important. They were right after all. Some young boys went by, arguing loudly. Behind them was Liliana, with that swaying gait of hers. She glanced at the table as if this was the first time she had seen it, lifted the tray with her left hand, and using her other hand wiped it with a wet cloth, even though there was no need because they hadn't made it dirty. As she was doing so, she said:

"We get all kinds of weirdos in here."

"Let's go," said Mao, suddenly standing up.

Lenin imitated her, and since in order to get out she needed Marcia to get up, she took her arm and helped her stand. Mao took the other arm, and the two of them pointed her toward the door. Serious, inscrutable, still holding the tray, Liliana kept staring at them until they were outside.

The cold air revived Marcia. It was not that cold, but the heat inside the Pumper had been too high and she could feel the contrast, especially because she had not taken off her sweater. By the time they had taken a few steps, her discomfort had vanished ... possibly because it had never really existed. She felt very lucid; her thoughts stirred and spread, even though there was still nothing to apply them to. This gave her a sense of completion. She felt that the moment was coming—in fact it was rushing toward her—to find a way to say good-bye to them. It was a kind of compulsion to think, for the moment in an imminent way, and Marcia knew that when her thinking presented itself as ideas, and the ideas as words, the contraction of the fullness would make the world a toy. In reality everything was becoming tiny. The street itself showed her this: all the lit streetlamps did was reduce the night to a kind of protective bubble from which it was impossible to escape as if from a dream. With a gesture very common to anyone leaving an enclosed space, she raised her eyes to the sky (to see if it was raining). She seemed to see the stars, or saw them absentmindedly, without thinking, which when it comes to stars was the same as not seeing them at all. Not much time had passed, because the activity in the street had not changed since they had gone into the Pumper. Most of the teens were still standing on the opposite sidewalk; on this side there were small groups on the steps of the bank next to the Pumper, but mostly everything was in motion. The traffic was so dense it made your head spin. The punks' rapid steps, which for some unknown reason she fell in with, only added to this sensation. The crush of people separated and then brought them back together within a few feet two or three times. Mao took her by the arm impatiently, and pulled her toward the triangular recess of a perfume shop. Lenin followed them.

"Wanna fuck? Say you do."

"Let go of me," said Marcia, frowning. "Start by taking your hands off me. The answer is no. It's still no: why would it change? I want to go home."

And yet she had come to a halt. But when she saw Mao's determined gesture, one she thought was crazy—shaking her head without taking her eyes off Marcia's (normally when somebody shakes their head to say no, they take their eyes off the other person) she felt an urgent need to keep on walking. She took a few steps back toward the sidewalk, and paused to collect her thoughts. Together with the desire to get away came a more powerful one to talk, because she suddenly felt she could do so, as if Mao's insistence on her main aim freed her from a spell.

"It was your fault we couldn't talk in there. We're in the same position as before, or worse. I wanted to know something, but I still don't have any idea about it. It may not be important to you, but what about me?"

"It's not important to you either."

"You're so stubborn! And inconsiderate!"

"We did as you wanted, but in fact there was no need to talk."

"In that case, there's nothing more to say. Bye."

She took off without looking back at them.

"Love isn't something to be talked about," said Mao.

"There are lots of things that can be talked about. It's all very complicated." Marcia had no idea what she was saying.

"No, it's very simple. You have to decide on the spot."

The other two had also started walking, very quickly as usual. The three of them were heading for the street corner. Mao seemed to be gathering strength for a decisive attack. Marcia decided she was no longer interested. She was fed up with the argument.

Far more than she admitted, more sincerely, Marcia was disappointed that the conversation had gone nowhere. Not so much because she had not learned anything about the world of punks (because as she had no idea what information there was, she couldn't know if they had told her a lot or a little) but because the punk world had not turned out to be a world backward, the symmetrical, looking-glass image of the real one, with all its values reversed. That would have been the simplest answer, one that would have left her satisfied. Marcia was a bit ashamed to admit this, because it was so childish, but she didn't want to make things any more difficult for herself. It, and everything else along with it, was a missed opportunity, and so she considered the matter closed.

They had reached the street corner; Mao came to a halt.

She peered along Calle Bonorino, which was in darkness, then turned to Marcia.

"Let's go along here a bit. There's something I want to tell you."

"No. There's nothing more to say."

"There's just one more thing, Marcia, but it's fundamental. Isn't it unfair to cut me off when I'm finally going to tell you the most important thing? Because now I do want to talk to you about love."

In spite of everything she had decided a moment earlier, Marcia was curious. She knew she would hear nothing new, but still she felt intrigued. This was the magic spell the punks had cast on her: they made her believe the world could be renewed. The disappointment was secondary. She was the one who added this element, but Marcia was one of those people who had the habit of disregarding themselves and evaluating the situation without taking themselves into account. So she followed Mao, and Lenin followed her. They didn't walk far. There was a dark stretch twenty meters further on beyond the lit shop windows of Harding's. The three of them huddled against the wall. Mao launched straight in, her voice urgent. She had her eyes fixed on Marcia who felt freer in the dim light to return her gaze with an intensity unusual in her.

"Marcia, I'm not going to tell you again that you're wrong, because you must know that by now. The big mistake is the world of explanations you live in. Love is a way out of that mistake. An escape from that mistake. Why do you reckon I can't love you? Do you have an inferiority complex, like all fatties? No. And if you think you do, you're wrong about that too. My love has transformed you. That world of yours is contained within the real world, Marcia. I'm going to take the trouble to explain a few things to you, but don't forget I'm talking about the real world, not the one of explanations. What's preventing you from responding to me? Two things: the suddenness and the fact that I'm a girl. I've nothing to say about the suddenness; you believe in love at first sight just as I do, and so does the rest of the world. That's a necessity. We can't do without that. Now, as for me being a girl and not a boy, a woman and not a man ... You're horrified at us being so brutal, but it hasn't occurred to you that in the end that's all there is. In those same explanations you're always looking for, when it comes down to it, when it's the very last explanation, what's left but a naked, horrible clarity? Even men are that brutal, even if they are professors of philosophy, because underneath everything else there's the length and breadth of their pricks. That and nothing more. That's the reality. Of course it may take them many years and many miles to realize that; they can exhaust every single word beforehand, but it's all the same, however long they take, whether it takes them a lifetime to get there, or if they flash their dick at you before you've even crossed the street. We women have the wonderful advantage of being able to choose the long or short route. We can turn the world into a stroke of lightning, the blink of an eye. But since we don't have dicks, we waste our brutality in contemplation. And yet ... *there is* suddenness. An instant when the whole world becomes real, when it undergoes the most radical change: the world becomes world. That's staring us in the face, Marcia. That's when all politeness, all conversation has to stop. It's happiness, and that's what I'm offering you. You'd be the most stupid cow of all time if you didn't see that. Just think, there's so little separating you from your destiny. You only have to say yes.'

Twice before Marcia had noticed something strange she could not define. Now she knew what it was. She understood, or put into words, something she had been aware of for a while, perhaps from the start: that Mao was beautiful. It struck you immediately. She was surprised she had not told herself so before now. She was the most beautiful girl she had ever seen. And more than that. To have a pretty face and harmonious features or an exquisite range of expressions was not that unusual among girls of her age. But Mao was much, much more. She went beyond whatever thoughts could be formulated about beauty: she was like the sun, like light.

And this wasn't an effect. It wasn't the kind of beauty discovered over a short or long time, out of habit or love or both these things together; it wasn't beauty seen through the lens of subjectivity or time. It was objective. It was real beauty. Marcia was sure of this because beauty had never meant much to her; she didn't even notice it or take it into account. Among her schoolmates there were several who could boast that they were perfect beauties. Compared to Mao, they were like illusions confronted with the real.

Okay, she told herself, so that was Mao's secret weapon, and everything could be explained from that starting point. But at the same time, that wasn't an explanation. Because how could beauty be a secret?

"And yet," Mao was saying, "love also allows for one detour, just one: action. Because love, which cannot be explained, does in fact have *proofs*. Of course, these are not exactly procrastination, because proofs are the only thing love has. And however slow and complicated they may be, they are also instantaneous. These proofs are as valuable as love, not because they are the same or equivalent, but because they open a perspective onto another aspect of life: action."

Marcia had paid no more attention to this part of Mao's speech than to what had come before. Her own reflections were also coming to a close: Mao's and her thoughts were like two parallel series, and this lent them a certain harmony. After verifying, or discovering, Mao's beauty, and still affected by an amazement she could not put a name to, Marcia turned to look at Lenin. What had just happened led her to see something she had not seen before. In fact, she had not looked either of them in the face before.

Lenin was no beauty. Or perhaps she was. She had a long, horsey face, and all her features (eyes, nose, mouth) seemed out of proportion, and haphazard. But in her entirety, she could not be called ugly. She was different. So different she made one think of a kind of beauty that might be appreciated in another civilization. She was the opposite of Mao. In an exotic, primitive or directly extraterrestrial court, her face could have been considered a living jewel, the realization of an ideal. Generations of incestuous monarchs would have been needed to produce her, and this would have led to dynastic struggles, intrigues, kidnappings, knights in strange armor, castles on the top of inaccessible hills ... Lenin too had something to discover, which for Marcia became real at that moment: the novelesque. There was also a deep-seated similarity to Mao: they were like the two faces of the same thing. Beauty and difference exploded in the night, and the transformation they were creating was not, unlike the others she had thought she had perceived (this one changed their nature) a turning of the page to a new version of the world, but *the transformation of the world into world.* It was the height of strangeness, and Marcia did not think she could get any further. She was right about this, because there were no more transformations; or rather, the situation took on the aspect and rhythm of one great transformation that was simultaneously hanging in midair and vertiginous. Marcia congratulated herself for having given them another chance, and even felt a retrospective, hypothetical fear: if she had done as she intended and gone home a few minutes earlier, she would have missed this discovery, which seemed to her fundamental. How often, she thought, from not making one tiny further effort, people lost the opportunity for positive and enriching lessons.

Mao was looking expectantly at her. Marcia looked back at her and had to shut her eyes (inwardly): she was too beautiful. She was on the verge of asking her to please repeat the question, if there had been a question, but Mao wasn't expecting a reply. On the contrary, it was as if she herself gave it:

"You'll have to prove yourself," she said.

Marcia had no idea what she was talking about, but nodded anyway. Then something extraordinary happened: Mao smiled. This was the first and only time she did so, and Marcia, who had absolutely no way of being certain this was a smile, knew beyond the shadow of a doubt that Mao had smiled at her.

In fact this was one of the rarest phenomena in the universe, the "serious smile," which men who are very lucky get to see once or twice in their lifetimes, and women practically never. It made her think, possibly by an association of names, of a photograph of Mao Tse Tung, one of those official photos in a blurred newspaper reproduction, where even with the best will in the world not even the keenest eye can decide if there is or is not the hint of a smile on the Chinese leader's face.

It was extremely fleeting, no more than an instant, and the punks were already off in search of their enigmatic "proof." Marcia gravitated to them naturally ... the gravitational pull of mystery, still lost in the mist of her thoughts, none of which (neither the one about beauty, nor the one about the novelesque, nor about the smile) had assumed a definite shape. They crossed the street without bothering to look whether a car was coming or not; on the far corner the darkness was deeper because it was an abandoned arcade. After a moment's hesitation when Mao headed toward Rivadavia, she changed her mind and said something to Lenin.

"Let's go!" she ordered, and strode off in the opposite direction. Marcia had heard them mutter the word *Disco*, and from the way it was said had understood they were going to the supermarket of that name. And yes, passing the cinema and a small bakery, they went into an arcade at the end of which was the enormous Disco supermarket, all lit up in neon. She had an intuition of what they were planning. As far as proofs of love went it was a classic gesture (a classic even though nobody had done it before): to steal something from a supermarket and give it her. The equivalent of what in olden days would have been the slaying of a dragon. Of course, she had no idea what it would prove, but she was ready to watch. Viewed from this century's enlightened present, anybody would say that dragons had never existed. But then again, for a medieval peasant, did supermarkets exist? In the same way, the proof that was still some distant possibility laid open the credit of existence. Would they ask her to wait outside? There were two massive glass walls separating the supermarket from the arcade. A lot of people were inside; all the cash registers were open, and there were long lines snaking between the displays that blocked everything. The main door was almost at the exit of the arcade on to Calle Camacuá. No, they weren't going to make her wait outside: without a word, Mao stepped aside so that Marcia could go in first. When she entered ... Not exactly the moment she entered, but when she looked back and saw what Lenin was doing when she came in ... was like the onset of a dream. And at the same time it was as if reality was starting.

From her bag, or possibly from among the metal objects hanging round her neck, Lenin had taken a heavy black iron padlock; she was closing the glass door, slipping the bolt and attaching the padlock. The click it made as it snapped shut made Marcia jump. It was as if the lock had literally shut on her heart. Or better still, as if her heart were the black iron padlock that was slightly rusty but still worked perfectly, too well in fact. Because the move had something irreversible about it (when a padlock closes it's as if it will never be able to be opened again, as if the key had somehow already been lost). Added to the surprise, this made it a dream come true ...

She was not the only one to have seen this. A short, elderly woman with white hair and a red coat had just reached the door to go out, pushing a piled-high shopping cart.

"Get back," Lenin told her, switchblade open in her palm.

A boy in a Disco t-shirt, who was helping load bags at the counter, took a few steps toward the intruder, but came to a halt when he saw the knife, his face almost comically reflecting his stupefaction. Lenin turned toward him, brandishing the blade:

"Stay still, you asshole, or I'll kill you!" she shouted. And to the old woman, who was rooted to the spot: "Get back to the cash register."

She stamped her foot on the ground, then with a swift movement stabbed at a carton of milk that was on top of the cart. A jet of white spattered several other women approaching the exit right in the eyes.

Almost at once, Lenin moved beside Marcia toward the

Fruit and Veg section, which faced the street. A man in a white apron came out from behind an electronic scale, as if he had taken control of the situation and was determined to put a stop to it. Lenin wasted no time on him. She thrust the knife at him, and when the man raised his arms to snatch it from her or to hit her, she slashed his face with lightning speed. The blade slit his cheek left to right, down to the bone, from the gum behind his upper lip. His whole top lip was left dangling, with blood spurting up and down. He had begun to shout something but never finished whatever it was. He raised both hands to his mouth.

All this had only taken a few seconds, scarcely long enough for anyone to realize what was happening. The women who were choosing fruit and vegetables in this section, which could not be seen from the rest of the supermarket, started to look alarmed, but Lenin was already trotting through them, knife dripping blood, toward the small counter at the back, where the girl receiving empty bottles stood rooted to the spot. Behind her was a small door which led to the delivery bay for trucks. Marcia, who had stayed near the front door, turned to get a better look at what Lenin was up to. She saw that she was heading for this other exit, to do the same as she had with the first one. This time it must be a metal shutter. She didn't doubt for a second that Lenin would lock it with another padlock ... Marcia simply hoped she had the keys, because otherwise she had no idea how they would get out of there, and in this situation the need to get out was uppermost in her mind; she couldn't think of anything else. But somehow inevitably what most characterized them, what was most like their way of burning their bridges, was for there to be no keys, that they were closing the padlocks forever.

At that moment, gunshots rang out over her head. Two, three or four of them: impossible to count. They were not all that loud, but the faces of those already alarmed snapped back. Incredibly, so far no one was shouting. To Marcia's left, against the walls giving on to the street and behind the electronic scale, stood a ladder. This area had a low ceiling. Up above hung a not very large goldfish bowl-cum-office, where obviously a guard was posted who could see every part of the supermarket. There was no closed-circuit TV or anything of that kind; the surveillance was on a primitive level, watchtower-style. Mao must have climbed the ladder while her friend was putting on the show with her knife, and by now must have overpowered the security guard. Overpowered or something worse: Marcia could have sworn he had not been the one to shoot.

In the deathly silence reigning in the Fruit and Veg section following the shots (all that could be heard through the loud-speakers was a jingle for instant mashed potato) the noise of the metal shutter to the adjacent delivery bay made a huge clang. It was such a conclusive sound that the padlock seemed unnecessary. To anyone else it would have seemed incredible that two young women could do things like shutting a metal shutter weighing tons, sidelining the dozen beefy truck drivers and porters who must have been in the delivery bay, or taking out one or two professional security guards and seizing their weapons ... But to Marcia it did not seem unbelievable; on the contrary, she wouldn't have believed anything else.

The echo of the metal shutter slamming had scarcely faded away (really, these girls didn't allow anyone's attention to wander) when all gazes turned to staring up at the office suspended under the ceiling, where one of the glass panels exploded. A hail of big and small shards of glass rained down on the aisle between Fruit and Veg and Soft Drinks. In the midst of them fell the projectile that had caused the damage, which was nothing other than a telephone, its cable torn out.

Then, in the hole the broken glass had created, Mao appeared, revolver in one hand and microphone in the other. She looked calm, self-assured, an imposing figure, in no hurry. Above all in no hurry, because she wasn't wasting a single moment. Things were happening in a packed continuum that they perfectly controlled. It was as if there were two distinct times operating simultaneously: the one the two punks were in, doing one thing after another without any gaps or pauses, and the other of the spectator-victims, where everything was gaps and pauses. The recording that had been coming over the loudspeakers had ceased, to be replaced by the sound of Mao breathing as she prepared to speak. This in itself caused widespread terror. Efficiency often has that effect. It must have been quite simple to cut the transmission of a recorded tape and replace it with a directly amplified voice: no more than pushing a button. But knowing how to do something easy is not easy. The entire clientele of the supermarket joining forces could have been pushing buttons for a whole week without succeeding. And they knew it, which made them feel they were at the mercy of an efficiency that asserted itself so effortlessly.

"Listen carefully, all of you," said Mao over all the loudspeakers in the store. She spoke slowly, carefully controlling the echoes. She had adopted a neutral tone, as though giving information, but it was pure hysteria. So great and pure that the growing hysteria among the customers of both sexes seemed like nothing more than an everyday attack of nerves. It led them to understand that it was not enough for their nervousness or fears to pile up and grow in order to become hysteria. This was something different. It was something that by definition did not grow, a paroxysm reached outside of life, madness or even fiction. As silence fell, the beeps from the last cash registers that had continued to work died away.

"This supermarket has been taken over by the Love Commando. If you collaborate, there will not be many injured or dead. There will be some, because Love is demanding. The number depends on you. We will take all the money in the cash registers, and then leave. Within a quarter of an hour, the survivors will be at home watching TV. That's all. Remember that everything that happens here will be a proof of *love*."

How literary she was! This was followed by one of those moments of hesitation that take place at the expense of the real in reality. A man in one of the lines guffawed. Immediately there was the sound of a gunshot, but instead of producing a hole in the forehead of the man who had laughed, the bullet hit the leg of a small woman who was two behind him in line. The leg began to spout blood, and the woman fainted melodramatically.

There was a huge commotion and shouting. Mao waved the recently fired revolver and raised the microphone to her lips again. White and shaken, the man stopped laughing. The shot had been intended for him. It was as if he were dead, because in the fiction relating to his earlier incredulity the bullet hole really was in his forehead.

"Everybody back," said Mao. "Move away from the cash registers; you cashiers as well. Stand between the shelves. I'm going to get down now. I'm not going to give you any more warnings." She tossed the revolver over her shoulder, using her free hand to feel for the things she was carrying round her neck. She picked out one, which looked like a small black metal pineapple, the size of a hen's egg. She said: "This is a nerve-gas grenade. If I let it off, you'll all be paralyzed and brain-dead for the rest of your lives."

There was a mass movement back. The people on the far side of the cash registers rushed through them. The cashiers abandoned their posts; supervisors, assistants, everyone piled up, trying to hide behind the shelves. Those who found the woman who had fainted in their way trampled on her and the spreading pool of blood around her body. There must have been about four hundred people of all ages and social groups as well as quite a few children, some of them babies in strollers. They pushed and shoved in their haste to get away, but what Mao said next stopped them in their tracks:

"Look over there," she said, pointing to her left. Lenin had appeared on top of the dairy counter, holding a bunch of gasoline cans in her hand. "Anyone trying to get out the back of the shelves will be burned alive."

The whole back wall of the store was covered with low meat freezers, a counter for cheeses and cold meats, and finally, separated by a narrow aisle, the dairy cabinet that Lenin was standing on. But beyond them was an empty area, in which employees of both sexes stood in white aprons, staring in astonishment at the back of the arsonist, who wasn't paying them the slightest attention. Why didn't they go for her? Most of them had not learned of Lenin's locking the delivery bay, and might have thought it was still open, with people inside who could come to their aid. And so two men, one of them smaller, the other huge and with a big belly rushed instinctively to grapple with Lenin, hoping to open a breach and head for the street exit. The fat guy, who must have thought he was a human locomotive, managed to climb up through the yogurts and reach out to the sentinel, who did not move. In the blink of an eye he was doused in gas, and a well-aimed kick sent him sprawling on his back. He had barely touched the ground when he burst into flames. Had she thrown a match at him? Nobody really saw. By now he was a flaming torch. His plastic overall caught fire spectacularly, and his cries echoed all round the supermarket. He was hit on the head by another gas can, and since this exploded on the spot, turning his brain into a fireball, he suddenly stopped screaming. Only slightly singed, his colleague did his best to hide among the others. Of all the shouts going up, curiously the most intelligible were those of the women who for their children's sake begged for the threat of nerve gas not to be carried out. Some things strike a chord in the imagination.

While this was going on, all the lights had gone off, as well as the red numbers on the cash registers, and the sound system. From her perch, Mao had cut off the electricity. In the sudden darkness (their eyes would take a few seconds to adjust and take advantage of the light from the arcade and street) the effect of the burning man and the vast pool of flaming fuel was dazzling.

But the two attackers did not seem to have to wait to get used to the darkness. They had done so earlier, and now they only had to act. Like a bat or nocturnal monkey, Mao dropped down from the office to the first of the cash registers. She began to leap from one to the next until she reached the furthest one. Curious onlookers had started to gather in the shopping arcade on the other side of the windows. They peered in without understanding what was going on.

Beyond the displays and the customers, the tearful, baying crowd (after all, they had been told to follow orders, but not to be quiet) Lenin was moving in the opposite direction of her friend, along the tops of the freezers, treading on meat and chickens. If this movement were not simply carried out to create an impression of symmetry, it could have no other motive than to dissuade and threaten. Everything seemed aimed at that: there was a threat, but not a simple, straightforward and comprehensible one, rather one confused with the realities it referred to, which in this way no longer functioned as a language but merged into a blurred, illegible whole. And yet a language did exist, because in the bilateral symmetry of their maneuvers Mao represented the ultimate intention: to steal the money from the cash registers, whereas Lenin was the threat that existed above and beyond their crimes, since she prevented any escape in the other direction. And she obviously did have something in mind, because she leaned over and gathered together the shopping carts close to the freezers and launched them toward the back of the store, toward the milk products and the wine shelves.

When she reached the last cash register, Mao began to empty it systematically. She did so without taking her feet from the counter where goods were put, simply bending from the waist up. She pressed the button that released the cash drawer, tore out the tray containing different compartments for change, scooped up the large-denomination banknotes underneath, and stuffed them into a plastic bag dangling from her wrist. This operation took her no more than a second or two; then she jumped across to the next cash register.

She was leaping from the second to the third cash register (and the spectators were only just beginning to realize what was going on) when an explosion rocked the supermarket, the arcade it was part of, the surrounding block, and doubtless the entire neighborhood. By some miracle, the panes of glass at the front were not blown out, but something even better occurred: they were shattered but stayed in place, turning opaque as though covered in vapor, and thwarting the curiosity

of the onlookers outside—most of whom had run off anyway
when they heard the noise, fearing the whole arcade might fall
in. The hostages' terror reached new heights. The explosion
had come from the delivery bay behind Lenin. It must have
been caused by a fuel tank. The sudden holes in the wall let in
light and the dreadful crackle of the fire. Almost immediately
there were another two explosions, perhaps from the trucks'
gas tanks. Although less deafening than the first, they were accompanied by the screech of bits of metal tearing apart. The
lights had gone out in the arcade as well, so that now the scene
was lit only by the dancing, flickering flames. Mao had not
paused, and by now had emptied another two registers. If it
crossed anybody's mind to take advantage of the darkness to
grab her, they must have thought twice about it, because the
entire wall between the store and the warehouse area now silently collapsed. Since everything was in flames on the far side,
the whole scene was bathed in an intense glow. One person
did not consider this properly, and threw herself at the thief.
She was a girl in a cashier's pink uniform; a robust, stocky and
obviously determined young woman. The sight of the fire had
spurred her on, or had led her to forget the precautions of only
a few seconds before. Maybe she thought her example would
lead to a general revolt. But that didn't happen. She ran straight
for Mao, who was leaning over a cash register. She charged like
a rhinoceros, as if this were a natural instinct in her, almost as
though she made a habit of it, as if in the past this maneuver

had always brought good results. Mao's reaction was instantaneous and very precise: she swayed backward, a bottle of wine in one hand, and brought it down in a wide arc at the very instant the chubby cashier reached her. It smashed on her forehead, and the crack of the poor girl's skull resounded round the store. It was a brutal death, but somehow in keeping with her bull-like charge. No one else tried to copy her. Despite this, Mao stopped what she was doing for a moment and surveyed the motionless crowd among the shelves. The light from the fire shone directly on her. She was so beautiful is sent shivers down the spine.

"Don't interrupt me again!" was all she said.

She let another second go by, like a schoolteacher might after reprimanding some unruly pupils, to see if there were any objection. The four hundred desperate hostages had none whatsoever. Without opening their mouths, they all seemed to be shouting: "We don't want to die!"

But one shrill voice was raised among the mass of shadows where madness might well be brewing.

Although shrill, it was a man's voice. With a very strong Colombian accent. From the first few syllables, many of those present realized what was going on. The neighborhood is itself an education. Two blocks from *Disco*, on the corner of Camacuá and Bonifacio, there was a Faculty of Theology that offered scholarships to students from all over Latin America. They stayed in apartments on the campus and shopped in the area. They were a kind of learned evangelists, with a touch of hippie. In a neighborhood like Flores, foreigners are always suspected of being indiscreet. It was almost inevitable that this Colombian should intervene.

"You don't scare me, Satan!" he began. And that was practically it.

Lenin had interrupted her maneuvers level with the space between shelves where the voice came from. In the opposite direction from Mao, she was silhouetted against the flames, which were very close to her. In her hand a transparent gas can shone like a gem. There were at least fifty people between her and the protestor, but that did not seem to deter her.

"Shut up, you idiot!" shouted one man. Shouts backing him up came from all around, demonstrating an unsuspected hatred of religion.

"The devil ..." shrieked the Colombian.

"What devil, for fuck's sake!"

"Shut up, why don't you?"

"Kill him, kill him!" a woman shouted. "For our children's sake! Kill him before there's another tragedy!"

And another woman, more philosophical:

"This is no time for sermons!"

In reality, the Colombian had not even begun any religious argument, but the others had sensed it coming anyway. In a neighborhood like Flores, everything gets known. And what isn't known is intuited. The first man who had shouted him down started punching him. There was a tremendous uproar, because the student, who ought to have been feeble, a member of a decadent race, defended himself. But none of this was visible in the darkness. Besides, there were outbreaks of hysteria elsewhere in the crowd. A controlled, cautious hysteria, because no one wanted to overstep the boundaries the attackers had set.

Even so, it did not look as if those boundaries would be respected for more than a few seconds. The fire was really terrifying, and gave the impression it would soon spread to the store itself. Besides, if one wall had collapsed, the roof might come down as well. Mao began her looting of the cash registers again, but seemed to be doing so more slowly now, half-expecting an attack, almost wanting to teach them another lesson.

The reasonable thing would have been for her to finish taking the money, and then for the attackers to flee. Nobody was going to stop them. But their initial warning echoed in the collective consciousness: if they were doing all this for love, something was missing, some fresh horror. Love could always do more.

In response to this plea, Lenin took a horrendous initiative. The tumult caused by the Colombian was still going on when the deafening sound of a shopping cart was heard, launched like a missile from one end to the other of the back aisle. Those close to it could see the cart was filled to the brim with bottles of champagne, and topped off with half a dozen cans of gasoline and an areola of blue flames. It sped straight down the aisle without touching anything, and crashed into one end of the soft drinks display. The blast was unparalleled; the shock wave a dense mass of green glass splinters and flaming alcohol. The impact also set off the rapid explosion of a thousand exploding soft drinks bottles. A lot of people had sought refuge among these shelves, and so the incident caused even greater chaos. It was as if the screams were reaching the highest heavens. Mao's movements between the cash registers had become supernaturally slow.

The confusion was so great it would be a shame not to take advantage of it, thought one woman who found herself in a convenient spot. She must have thought: what are we waiting for? If this is a nightmare, let's behave the way we do in dreams. Mao had advanced across six or seven registers already. She was a long way from the first ones, and that must have settled it as far as this impatient woman was concerned. She sprinted as fast as she could from the shelves to the gap between the first and second cash register. She raced through and in the blink of an eye was up against the window facing the arcade. If she had put her shoulder to it, she would have got out: it was only by some miracle or other that the completely shattered glass stayed in place. It would not have resisted a determined shove. But the woman, either stunned or crazy, wanted to take the logic of dreams that had brought her this far to its inevitable conclusion: kneeling down in front of the plate glass window, she began cutting it with the diamond in her ring. The circle she started to trace was far too small for her body, but that was the least of her problems. In two bounds, Mao had come up behind her, but nobody saw exactly what she did among the madly dancing shadows. It barely lasted an instant. In the first half of this short lapse of time, the woman managed to scream loudly; in the second, supreme half, she fell quiet, and with good reason. When her attacker straightened up, like a modern Salome dressed in black, she was holding the woman's head in her hands. The spectacle attracted everyone's attention. The hubbub intensified, and what emerged out of it, more than the cries of "Murderer! Animal! and so on, were the "Don't look!" that everybody was urging everyone else to do. This was the second half of what was dreamt: the fear of dreaming, or of remembering, which is the same thing. But Mao had leapt up onto the counter closest to her, and threw the head like a bowling ball at the shouting crowd.

As the severed head traced an arc through the air in which all the brutal light and darkness of the fire was vividly etched, a second cart behind the backs of the spectators was dispatched in the opposite direction to the first. A fresh blast set off a third fire against the back wall of the store, where the thoughtful shelves of wine were kept. It became impossible to breathe, as the fire's intense heat was filled with acrid smells. Everything edible or drinkable in the supermarket was added to the concoction. The household cleaning department adjacent to the soft drinks area had also caught fire. The containers of solvents, waxes, polishes, and ammonia went up with a choking stench. The trapped crowds tried to get away, trampling on each other, showing no solidarity, each one desperate to save themselves. Whole shelves began to give way on top of people. And the woman's head was still in midair, not because it had come to a standstill in a miraculous postmortem levitation, but because only a very short space of time had elapsed.

In the darkness of the flames, in the crystal of smoke and blood, the scene was multiplied in a thousand images, and each of these thousand in a thousand more … realms of weightless, rootless gold. It was as if at last there was a kind of understanding of what was going on. There is an old proverb which says: If God does not exist, everything is permitted. But the fact is that everything is never permitted, because there are laws of verisimilitude that survive the Creator. Even so, the second part of the proverb can function, that is, become reality, hypothetically at least, giving rise to a second proverb on the same lines as the original: If everything is permitted … This new proverb does not have a second part. Indeed, if everything is permitted … then what? This question was projected onto the thousand confused contours of the panic in the supermarket, and found some sort of reply. If everything is permitted … everything is transformed. It is true that transformation is also a question; on this occasion however, it became a momentary, shifting affirmation; it did not matter that it was still an interrogative, it was also an answer. The incident had illuminated, even if in the shadows, the amazing potential for transformation latent in all things. A woman, for example, a local housewife who had gone to buy food for supper, was melting on the spot in full view of her neighbors, who paid no attention to her. The fire had caught the viscose of her padded coat, and she had turned into a monster, but a dancing monster, lending her a voluptuousness she had never possessed when she was alive. Her limbs were elongated—one hand at the end of a three-meter long arm was crawling across the floor, a leg twisted and twisted endlessly on itself like a cobra ... And she was singing, without opening her mouth, in a voice that would have left Maria Callas sounding flatulent and fuzzy, while at the same time the song was enriched by inhuman laughter, panting and prancing ... she became animal, but all animals at once, an animal spectacle, with the bars of her cage sticking out like spines from every fold of her body, an animal jungle weighed down with orchids. A torrential rainbow spread over her: red, blue, snow white, green, dark gloomy green ... She became vegetable, a stone, a stone colliding, the sea, an octopus automaton ... she murmured, acted (Rebecca, an unforgettable woman) declaiming her lines while also becoming a mime artist, a planet, a crackling candy wrapper, an active and passive expression in Japanese ... and at the same time she was no more than a gaze, a tiny insistence. Because the same thing could happen to anyone, and in fact did; she was only one instance among hundreds, a picture at an exhibition.

Mao was still busy and either because she had been so diligent or because the time had arrived, she was coming to the end of the cash registers. The bag she was holding in her left hand was stuffed with money. How much time had elapsed?

Five minutes in total since they had burst into the supermarket?
And so much had happened! They were all waiting for the police or the firemen, but knew this was merely an atavistic habit,
because there was nothing to wait for. What they felt was the
opposite of someone coming to help: the general atmosphere
was a centrifugal force, the Big Bang, the birth of the universe.
It was as if everything known was dispersing at the speed of
light, to create in the far distance, in the blackness of the universe, new civilizations based on other premises.

It was a beginning, but also the end. Because Mao, her job
done, leaped down from the first register, and Lenin joined her.
Together, the two of them threw themselves at the corner of
the window giving onto the street with the untouchable force
of love. The glass shattered and they vanished cleanly through
the hole ... two boundless dark shapes swallowed up by the im-
mensity of the world outside ... and at the very moment they
disappeared, a third shadow joined them ... Three stars whirl-
ing in the vast rotation of the night ... the Three Marias that all
the children of the southern hemisphere peer up at, spellbound,
uncomprehending ... and were lost on the streets of Flores.

MAY 27, 1989